BETWEEN THE STARS

Another You Say Which Way Adventure
by:

DM POTTER

ISBN-13: 978-1518811753
ISBN-10: 1518811752

How This Book Works

- This story depends on YOU.

- YOU say which way the story goes.

- What will YOU do?

At the end of each chapter, you get to make a decision. Turn to the page that matches your choice. **P62** means turn to page 62.

There are many paths to try. You can read them all over time. Right now, it's time to start the story. Good luck.

Oh ... and watch out for the shape shifting plants!

BETWEEN THE STARS

In the spaceship

You are in a sleep tank on the space ship *Victoria*. Your dreaming cap teaches you as you float.

You first put on a dreaming cap for the space sleep test. Although you thought it looked like you had an octopus on your head, you didn't joke about it. Nobody did. Everyone wanted to pass the test and go to the stars. Passing meant a chance to get out of overcrowded Londinium. If you didn't pass you'd likely be sent to a prison factory in Northern Europa. Nobody wanted to go there, even though Britannica hasn't been a good place lately, Europa was said to be worse.

When the judge sentenced you to transportation for stealing that food, you sighed inside with relief. You knew transportation was the chance of a better life on a faraway planet, but only if you passed the sleep test.

You lined up with other hopefuls and waded into a pool of warm sleep jelly. They were all young like you and they all looked determined.

"Stay calm," the robot instructed. "Breathe in slowly through your mouthpiece and relax."

Nearby, a young woman struggled from the pool. She

pulled out her breathing plug and gasped for breath.

"Take her back," said a guard. You knew what that meant – back to prison and then the factories. A convict sneered at the poor girl, the cruel look on his face magnified by a scar running down one cheek.

In your short time in prison, you had learned there were people who would have been criminals no matter what life they'd been born to. Something told you that he was one of them.

You put him out of your mind and concentrated on doing what the robot said. You thought of the warm porridge you'd had every morning in the orphanage growing up. The sleeping jelly didn't seem so strange then. When your head was submerged you breathed in slowly.

As the jelly filled your lungs you fought against thoughts of drowning. You'd listened at the demonstration and knew it was oxygenated. *This must be what it's like to be a fish*, you'd thought as you moved forward through the thick fluid, *I only have to walk through to the other side.*

Closing your eyes, you moved forward through the thick warm jelly. *Relax*, you told yourself. *You can do this.*

You opened your eyes just in time to see the scar-faced youth about to knock your breather off. Thankfully the jelly slowed his punch and you ducked out of the way just in time. Then a moment later, you were on the other side being handed a towel.

"This one's a yes," intoned a man in a white coat. He

slapped a bracelet on your wrist and sent you down a corridor away from your old life. As you exited, you just had time to hear the fate of the scar-faced youth. "He'll do. Take him to the special room."

Days of training followed. You often joined other groups of third class passengers but you didn't see Scar-Face among them. You passed all the tests and then one day, you got into a sleep tank beside hundreds of others. Your dreaming cap would teach you everything you'd need to know in your new life.

You were asleep when the *Victoria* was launched into space. You slept as the *Victoria* lost sight of the Earth and then its star, the sun.

And here you are, years later, floating in sleep fluid and learning with your dreaming cap. Or you were. Because now you hear music. Oxygen hisses into your sleeping chamber and the fluid you have been immersed in starts to drain away. Next time you surface, you'll breathe real air, something that your lungs haven't done in a long time.

"Sleeper one two seven six do you accept this mission? Sleeper, please engage if you wish to awaken for this mission. Sleeper, there are other suitable travelers for this mission. Do you choose to wake?"

Passengers can sleep the entire journey if they want. They can arrive at the new planet without getting any older. First class passengers will own land and riches when they arrive but you are third class, you have nothing. Groggily, you listen to the voice. If you choose to take on a mission you can earn credit for the new planet – even freedom – but you could also arrive on the new planet too old to ever use your freedom.

"Sleeper, do you accept the mission?"

It is time to make your first decision.

Do you want to wake up and undertake this mission? **P5**
Or

Do you wait for a different mission or wait to land on the new planet? **P121**

Wake up and undertake a mission

Light filters into your sleeping tank from above, changing the fluid around you into a blurry rainbow. The breathing tube sends you chemicals to bring you fully awake.

You wonder how long you've slept and what you've been learning. Sleepers need new information to keep their brains alive. In your sleep you might have learned about medicine, robotics, farming, steam engineering, aviation or anything else the makers of the *Victoria* need third class passengers to know.

A pang of homesickness hits you, but you remind yourself how lucky you were to get a place on the *Victoria* instead of going to the prison factories. There was nothing for you on Earth.

The last phase of waking begins. Soon you will be using your own lungs and walking the halls of the spaceship. There is enough light now to see the shapes of other tanks around you with their sleepers inside. The ship must not have landed if they are only waking you.

"Sleeper, prepare to exit your chamber."

As the last of the fluid drains out of the tank, you feel air against your skin and you wonder what space will be like. You hope the electrodes attached to your body have been doing their job stimulating your muscles. If they have, you'll be strong and fit. If not, you'll move like some sort of space slug, with your muscles wasted away from lack of exercise.

Something stirs outside. It's a robot shaped like a person.

The hatch of your sleep tank opens with a hiss. There is almost no gravity and small globules of the last of the sleep jelly float up ahead of you. A small bird-shaped robot flies about collecting the excess fluid through its long beak. The hummingbot's wings are a blur as it sucks up each bubble-like blob. Large green eyes scan about for the next one.

You hold onto a ladder on the side of the tank and pull yourself up. Being almost weightless makes it easy.

"May I assist you?" purrs the helpful voice of the robot as it waits nearby. It is a butler robot. Rich people had them in their houses on Earth. You've read in history books that some people used to be butlers but that robots replaced them. They don't need to sleep or rest and they don't steal your valuables. They also don't need to be paid.

The butler hands you a thick toweling tunic. From your training you know you need to get cleaned up and find some proper clothes. Your legs are a little wobbly but you don't really need them yet. You push off in low gravity and float towards the exit. Your body rises and you look across a warehouse of hundreds of other sleepers all looking like specimens in a museum.

You drift past rows and rows of people frozen at about the age of fourteen. Some have their eyes open but they don't see you. They are deep in space sleep. Some are moving, with electrodes stimulating them to do exercises that keep their bodies healthy. Some seem to be working at invisible tasks. All are learning. Each mind is slowly becoming an encyclopedia of special information.

While you enjoy being weightless and the sense of flying, the butler wheels along below you on a magnetic strip set into the floor. When you reach the end of the room you pass your palm over a door sensor and head into a ready room.

This room has artificial gravity. After such a long period of weightlessness, your limbs feel heavy and you move slowly. You take a quick shower to remove the oily covering all sleepers are coated in to preserve their skin. Then, when you're clean, you put on the uniform that the butler has laid out for you.

You look at your reflection in the mirror. You still *look* young but you are now much, much older in Earth years, and much wiser because of all the learning you've done. Space-sleep preserves youth. Many years ago rich people would pay to be kept in sleep chambers in the hopes that their medical problems could be solved while they slept. Wealthy criminals sometimes paid to sleep away their sentences. Now it's the way to travel between the stars. One-way time travel, some people call it.

Again, you wonder why you've been woken. In theory, the journey to a new planet can be accomplished without waking anyone, the robots take care of most things. But there are times when travelers like you can be woken. If other life forms are detected, the robots will wake people to assess the situation. You could also be called on if the ship experiences some mechanical failure. The ship needs to consult with its passengers if a course change is required. You doubt you'd be woken for that sort of thing; you aren't anyone important enough to make that sort of decision.

"Hey! Are you in there? Sleeper one two seven six? Or whatever your number is."

The voice comes from a little intercom beside the next door and doesn't sound like a robot. It sounds like a real person, just like you.

You press the connecting button and identify yourself to whoever is on the other side: "Traveler one two seven six reporting for duty."

You sound very formal compared to the speaker, but this is what you're supposed to say. It seems a good idea to follow the rules.

"That's great one-two. My name is Trig. If you're feeling like I did when I woke up you'll be itching to know why you're awake. I've brought a 'sporter down to meet you. We can ride to the briefing."

The gravity in this room feels like treacle to move through – you know it's a reaction from the sleep chamber. You're grateful there's a transporter out there for you. You'll have to build up your strength before you can walk far on your own.

You glance in the mirror one last time before you leave the room. You have no personal items, just your memories of Earth and a future ahead of you. The face in the mirror is the same one that entered the space ship at the beginning of the voyage. You smooth down your uniform and rub your fingers through your close-cropped hair.

You feel nervous, but you're excited too – you're about to meet another human being for the first time on this journey. Together you'll share an adventure that the descendants of all the travelers on board might recount one day. With thoughts of glory on your mind, you turn the big brass wheel and open the air lock between the two rooms. The seal opens with a hiss and you step through the portal to find yourself face to face with your new ship mate.

Trig has red hair and freckles. He looks the sort of boy who, when back on Earth, would have darted between carriages carrying messages about town for a few coins. The sort who could have helped out by holding a horse's reins or, just as easily, picking pockets. That's probably how he ended up on the *Victoria,* you think.

He wears a space uniform just like your own but he seems to have gotten it rather grubby and to have made a few modifications – whether for comfort or artistry you can't be sure. Trig isn't quite what you expected but then, you remind yourself, your previous lives probably weren't all that different. You come from an orphanage, you ended up in trouble and you don't look very old either. You've been sleeping and learning just as he has.

Trig leaps astride the transporter and motions for you to

join him. It's an electrified bicycle. It can be pedaled as you recall from your training, or it can draw from a reserve of stored power when needed.

Trig slaps the seat behind him and smiles. "Jump on!"

Trig pedals the 'sporter for a few yards and then flicks a switch. The bike leaps forward as the battery power kicks in.

You hold on tight, looking around the ship as the two of you zip along. The hallways are so wide that three horses could walk through them side by side. You see airlocks at intervals along the walls. Most have signs on them. They lead to storage warehouses, more sleepers, workshops and other facilities. The ship is carrying nearly one thousand men and women as well as animals. Everything needed to start a new colony is stowed on board and the ship itself is designed to be an initial shelter for settlers.

As Trig pulls up to a doorway, you see a butler wheeling along a magnetized strip on the floor. In the absence of gravity these strips keep the robots on track. Above your head a small flock of hummingbots fly by. They don't need the magnetic paths as their tiny clockwork motors can fly in any direction. They can even manage short excursions outside the ship.

"Where are we headed?" you ask, as Trig gets the 'sport moving even faster down a more ornate hall.

"To see the Captain." he says over his shoulder.

He doesn't need to yell, the ship is quiet and the 'sport whirrs along almost silently. The next corridor you enter seems more like something from a grand house than a spaceship. There are gleaming brass fittings around the doorways and inlaid designs on the walls and floors. Holographic frames display portraits of different people dressed in fine clothes. There are also scenic pictures of Earth – castles in Britannica, the Queen's palace in Londinium, mountains, lakes and other places you don't recognize. You wonder if the pictures are active when everyone is asleep or if they were just switched on for you and Trig.

The ship's port holes are normally closed while traveling at warp speed and its hull protected by layers of polymer metals shaped like feathers to withstand heat and cold.

Feathers! Wait, that's something *new* you've learned while sleeping. In your mind's eye you see pictures of a giant bird-like space ship covered in thousands of metallic feathers made from various metals that together, make a perfect shield against heat and cold.

Your thoughts are interrupted as the 'sporter pulls up to an important looking door. A brass sign reads 'BRIDGE'. The door has a carved border depicting the leaves of different trees. You recognize oak leaves but you aren't sure about the rest. You can't have learned any botany while you slept.

As Trig reaches towards the button he has a serious look on his face. "The Captain might not be what you're expecting

"What do you mean?" you say.

"You'll see."

A mental picture of what you think a Captain would be like flashes into your mind. He might be a tall man with a beard, perhaps someone from the military.

Trig busies himself turning the mechanism for the door. It swings open and you step through into the large operations room. Wide desks inset with navigation and monitoring equipment and several robots hum about the room. A special portal on the far wall displays a view of space outside. You can see stars and the never ending night. A young woman's voice interrupts your thoughts.

"I trust you woke well."

You turn to see a girl of about 15 or 16 standing in the centre of the room. She has long black braided hair arranged in a coil on top of her head. It is a simpler style than aristocrats wear on Earth, yet her hair tells you she is high born. You can't quite think why she is awake and not sleeping with the rest of the aristocracy. Then you realize what Trig was trying to tell you. This girl *is* the Captain.

"Ca—Captain, Sir. Reporting for du—duty," you stammer.

The Captain laughs at your nervousness and you feel yourself blushing. She crosses the room and extends her hand, smiling,

"Well, you took the idea of a female captain better than your crewmate there. My name is Helena Gillian Wells, and

I've been sleeping for one hundred and seventy years, as have you. It seems the robots have picked me to lead this mission. Nobody programmed them to make a distinction about gender. It is the start of a brave new sort of world, after all. So here we are. A small crew gathered to undertake a big mission."

Captain Wells walks into the middle of the room and gives you and Trig a run-down of the problem you were awakened to solve.

"The magnetic field surrounding the ship has been compromised. We need to find out what is wrong and fix it."

"Why do we need a magnetic field?" asks Trig. He looks from you to the Captain. You find yourself answering him:

"Space is full of harmful radiation, Trig. On Earth, the planet's magnetic field protects it. But here on the ship we have to generate our own magnetic field to keep everyone inside safe."

As you talk about magnetic fields and spaceship design you realize this must be something you've learned while sleeping. It's exciting to find out you know about how the ship works. You hope you'll know enough to fix whatever has gone wrong. This is a serious problem.

It's also an urgent problem. You need more information quickly so you can decide what to do. You walk over to the instruments that will give you radiation readings and make a scan of the dials.

"How safe are we now?" asks the Captain.

"The sleepers are fine," you say. "The sleep chambers are deep inside the ship. It's a bit like being underground. The hydroponic garden systems might be at risk though. I need to take some readings."

You walk over to the engine monitor and sit down to scan the information it's giving you. The engines are behaving normally but they are using more power than usual. The ship's protective magnetic field is weaker than it should be. Something is interfering with it.

"Is there a way we can get a view of the ship from the outside?" you ask.

"We can send out some hummers to scan," replies the Captain, "but we'll need to slow right down."

"I was going to recommend we do that anyway," Trig says, "the amount of power we're using isn't sustainable."

The Captain glares at him.

"When were you going to tell me that?"

Trig looks a little embarrassed.

"I wanted another techie to talk with before I said anything, I didn't want to upset you."

"Let's get something straight," Captain Wells says with a seriousness that shows she really is older than she looks, "I'm your Captain and I need to know *anything* regarding the optimal running of this ship. Is that understood?"

You and Trig start swapping notes. While you're talking, you keep discovering that you know more and more. Trig is having the same experience. It's exciting for both of you.

The Captain heads to a big control panel and starts working too. She confidently manipulates dials that give her readings about the different power sources on the ship. You wonder if she'll also be able to access messages sent from Earth while you've been traveling.

Trig slows the ship down and sends an order for five hummers to assemble at an exit port ready to go and look outside. One of the hummers begins to act as your eyes. It transmits images of the robot crew to you on a section of the big screen in the bridge. You also call up a spider-bot. If something needs fixing, the spider-bot will do the job. It can carry a large number of tools, has strength and agility, and its many arms enable it to hold on to the ship at the same time as carrying out repairs. The spider-bot is about the size of a small dog with a round central 'body' that holds tools. Its many arms allow you to perform remote mechanical work and its many eyes let you see all around it.

You and Trig go through a checklist of all the tools the spider-bot should carry. Trig calculates the flight path for each bird. Navigation is his specialty.

"Would you like me to check your calculations?" Captain Wells asks. Without waiting for Trig's reply she uploads the hummer's instructions to her display and looks them over. Trig bristles a bit. You suspect he doesn't like the idea of a high-born girl looking over his work.

You think things are a bit different now. Back on Earth,

an aristocratic girl's job is to look good, make a good marriage, and then organize social events and run her grand house. On the new planet there won't be a lot of entertaining, and the marriage market might be a lot simpler. Captain Wells, and women like her, are going to face big changes on the new planet.

Judging by Trig's first reactions to having a girl in charge, there might be some resistance to changing some of the old ways.

Meanwhile the Captain has been surveying the plans. "How about you arc the flights out *here* and *here*," she says. "Your trajectories are well plotted but I think we'd do well to scan as much of the surrounding sector as we can. This is a part of space we don't know much about."

Trig nods. "You're absolutely right Captain. I was so focused on checking the externals of the ship I didn't think about looking over our shoulder."

You think about how you can improve the plan too. "I can place some scanners on top of the spider-bot," you say. "If there's anything we want to take a better look at, we can get the bot to move into position. It won't run out of fuel like the hummers."

"Great idea," says Trig.

The two of you head down to get the bots ready. You take your own transporter this time. You'll need extra room to collect things. As you ride down a service corridor you feel a rush of exhilaration. On Earth your life was hard work and pretty dull. Now you are hurtling down a corridor to set up robots to go outside into a part of space nobody has explored before.

Waking up between the stars has risks. On this mission there's the threat of radiation poisoning for a start, but you'd rather be awake and dealing with it than sleeping through in ignorance. First class passengers don't want to get old. Space traveling takes a long time and they want to be able to get to a new planet and live there for a long time.

You round a corner and come to a long straight section of corridor.

"Race?" asks Trig with a glint in his eye.

It is time to make a decision.

Do you want to race around the Victoria on the transporters? **P18**

Or

Get on with the mission? **P59**

'Sporter vs 'sporter – racing in space

"Let's do it," you say.

You're sure you won't jeopardize the mission with a bit of fun. The magnetic field is still holding up and you've slowed the ship down. What could go wrong?

The two of you work out a course that will take you the long way around to the equipment rooms to the exit port. You jump on your transporters and countdown:

"Five, four, three, two, one, go!"

You squeeze the transporter's throttle and accelerate smoothly. The corridor becomes a blur. You stare ahead, keeping the machine on a slight lean as you race down the giant circular path.

When a sharper corner comes up, Trig manages to pull ahead as you slow down, fearing you'll lose balance, but the magnetic strips keep you firmly glued to the floor. Watching Trig lean into the next corner, you do the same, opening up the transporter a little more.

As you come to a long straight, you draw level with him. You look at each other and grin wildly. Other corridors and rooms flash by.

When both transporters suddenly lose power and come to a halt, you realize you've used up all the stored energy and will have to pedal the rest of the way. Then the hummingbots catch up. You're sure they could have flown faster but they have been content to plod along. They are programmed not to waste power.

"How far have we come?" you ask some time later. It feels like you've been pedaling for an hour. Sweat drips off your forehead, despite the cool temperature inside the spaceship.

Trig groans, looking at the corridor names. Each is named for a different explorer.

"We've passed Columbus, Cook and Drake. That looks like Livingstone coming up. I think we're more than half way. The equipment room is in Magellan."

"It would have been easier if whoever designed this ship had given the corridors numbers," you grumble as you pump the transporter's pedals. "This is pretty good exercise though." You feel your body working strongly. You haven't lost your strength while you slept. In fact you might be stronger than when the *Victoria* took off.

As you pass different corridors you have time to look at pictures of different explorers. A small screen on your bike tells you about each one as you pass, and what lies behind some of the different doors.

All sorts of things have been stockpiled on the ship to help build the new settlement. There is mining equipment, steam engines and the components of dirigibles for airborne exploration. There are entire rooms holding seeds so you can grow crops and there are plant warehouses where plants are grown to help oxygenate the air of the space ship and recycle the waste. It must have taken The Inventor and his workers years of thinking and planning to ready this expedition – they knew there would never be any going back.

You get to Magellan just as the transporters are fully recharged. Captain Wells is standing there and she looks very angry.

"What took you so long? I finished everything I had to do and came down to see how you were going with the bots and you haven't even started!"

"Hold your horses -" begins Trig, but he's cut short by the spaceship rolling and lurching. Gravity cuts out and you find yourself floating off the floor. Thankfully the 'sport stays stuck to the magnetic strip so you grab its handles. You know you need to get to an oxygen supply in case that cuts out too.

"Into an emergency room!" shouts Captain Wells, pulling herself along to a doorway. You grab onto picture frames and door handles to follow her. It's extremely bumpy and you bang into light fixtures several times. You're going to have a few bruises. The hummers shoot forward in spurts using a gas reserve for propulsion.

In short time you haul yourselves into a room with *EMERGENCY* stenciled in gold on the door. Inside you find a round room with padded walls covered in rich green velvet to protect you from the lurching motions of the ship. There is a circle of padded seats surrounding a central table. This looks like some sort of escape pod which could detach itself from the rest of the ship if necessary.

Captain Wells sits and reaches for belts tucked into the upholstery. She snaps the buckles closed to keep herself attached to the furniture. You do the same.

Whoever designed this ship made the emergency room just as beautifully as the rest of the ship. The table is intricately inlaid with command information and screens. The seats are comfortable and the ceiling is patterned.

The Captain sits at a smaller version of the controls on the bridge. You activate your own console and begin to monitor the *Victoria's* engines.

You can hear rattling and banging outside the emergency room and you are grateful for the straps that keep you in your seat. You think about all the equipment you passed on your circuit of the ship. Will it be damaged? You check the readings for the cargo holds and see the gravity has been diverted to all the priority areas – sleeping passengers and heavy equipment. Captain Wells and Trig are both studying readouts too.

"The dials are showing a high speed – but *we* aren't the ones doing the moving," says Trig, "it's like we're being sucked into something. I'll do my best to keep track of our course, but at the moment we're flying blind down some sort of rabbit hole."

"I've tried to close all the port holes," Captain Wells says, with steely determination. "But one won't shut. I'm going to bring it up on screen. We can at least take a look out of it."

An image appears in the centre of the table. You squint at the constellation you are viewing. It isn't familiar, but your knowledge of the stars is sketchy. Trig looks up from his navigation equipment:

"I've got good news, more good news and, depending on how you look at it, a spot of bad news."

Before you can offer an opinion about which news you'd like Trig to deliver first, Captain Wells thumps the table.

"Just make a full report and stop wasting time."

She looks at you both as she says it.

You blush, remembering you are partly at fault for this situation too. If you hadn't been racing around the ship instead of fixing it your ship might not have been sucked into this hole in space.

"Well Captain, we've stopped moving so fast and we're under our own power again such as it is, but we're completely lost. This area of space doesn't relate to any mapped constellations I know. I've tried steering us back toward the corridor we came through, but until we have more power, I wouldn't risk doing anything else."

You look at Trig. "And this is good news?"

Trig smiles "It's actually fantastic news. See that bright yellow star?" He stabs a finger onto his console leaving a bit of a smear on the glass. "That star has four planets circling it and at least two of them look to have the right conditions to support life!"

Captain Wells does a most un-captainly thing. She

unbuckles her seatbelt, boosts herself over to Trig and kisses him. Then she turns and gives you a hug. "We've still got a porthole that won't close and a problem with our magnetic field. Get the robot crew together and sort it out. Okay? While you do that, Trig can figure out which of these planets is our best bet."

You leave them studying the new solar system and head to the Magellan room to ready up the spider-bot and hummers. As you enter, the spider-bot runs toward you and opens its tool case. Each tool inside has to be attached to the case in two places so they don't float away into space when the box is opened. You add everything you think will be needed and then get the hummers to fill themselves with methane. They will be able to manage short flights by burning the fuel but they won't be able to fly in space using their wings like they do in the ship.

As each bird takes in the gas it turns an iridescent blue. The little robots carry small optical relays which will give you an aerial view of the ship. You remember the Captain's idea of a larger optical relay and fit one of the hummers with one. The hummer is barely able to fly so you create a perch on the spider-bot where it can sit until it is outside the ship in zero gravity.

The robot menagerie follows you to an airlock. You open the first door and usher them in. They line up, ready to go outside, just like pet dogs and cats would do. You step out of the chamber and close the door. You feel a slight vibration as the air lock opens, releasing the bots into space. The hummers fly with quick bursts from their methane powered jets. The spider bot uses suction cups and pincers to cling to the hull as it moves around.

Once you've closed the outer hatch you head back to meet Trig and carry out the inspection.

Trig and the Captain have made progress plotting a course to the first of the planets.

"The closest planet is really marginal," Trig says. "It's close enough that we can tell there isn't a lot of plant life. The ones that are further away look more promising. It's a big solar system though."

"Should we wake someone else up to help explore the planets?" you ask.

"They'll just want to pull rank on the Captain because she's a girl," says Trig. You remember all those corridors named after explorers. Were any named after a woman?

"That might be true," you say, "but we have protocols about waking up the aristocrats when a useful planet is found."

"But we don't really know that yet," Trig points out.

Captain Wells stands with her hands on her hips and looks at the screen which shows the robots outside.

"When you two have finished discussing the dangerous subject of mutiny, perhaps you should focus on fixing this ship. Besides, the robots will wake up The Inventor whether we choose to or not."

Trig blushes and you busy yourself sending the spider-bot instructions.

The hummers orbit the *Victoria* and show you what is happening. One area of the ship seems to have suffered some minor damage – there is space dust, probably from the passing tail of a comet, embedded in the feather-like covering of the ship.

The feathers shield the ship when entering a planet's atmosphere and generate an artificial magnetic field to protect from radiation. The dust has stopped some of them from working properly. You set the hummers to work, sucking up the dust while the spider makes any necessary adjustments.

"I've spent a hundred and seventy years in sleep school learning to be a cleaner and bird groomer," you say with a chuckle. "Hey Trig, how far out can the hummingbots go before we lose their signal?"

"Millions of miles. Why?"

"We could send some hummers out to scout the two planets. I think I can reconfigure them to get through the atmosphere and fly around the planets. That would give us an idea about which we should choose."

"Great idea," says Captain Wells. "That could save years of investigation. Tell me more when we've sorted this current problem. How is the magnetic field reading now?"

You check. "The magnetic field is almost back at 100 percent."

"Just as well," the Captain says. "We can't land without it."

"The feather protection is working perfectly again Captain," you report. "The bots also fixed the malfunctioning portal shutter. More space dust."

Captain Wells nods then stares out into space. You follow her eyes. This part of space is a deep purple, not the black you expected. It must be the effect of having a sun nearby.

"Let's follow through with this idea of some hummers taking an excursion to these new planets," the Captain says, looking at you and Trig. "Get the birds ready as soon as you can."

You and Trig head back to Magellan to pick up the spider-bot and the hummers. When they are back inside you carry out tests on the space dust.

"Blow me down," you say. "This dust is pure platinum."

"What's platignum?" asks Trig.

"Platinum's a very precious metal, more precious than gold. It's very odd to think of a cloud of it floating through space. Maybe it wasn't from a comet after all. I think I can set up some sensors for this sort of thing – it played havoc with our magnetic field and could have caused us to get radiation poisoning."

"What are you going to do with the dust?" Trig asks. He hefts the box. It's surprisingly heavy, the little spider bot was weighed down by it once it entered the low gravity of the spacecraft.

"How about we store it somewhere with our names on it," you suggest. "Perhaps we could use it in the future?"

"Excellent suggestion." Trig gives you a big smile. "It might get us out of a few years' work." He takes the box off while you busy yourself checking over the robots and readying them to make a long journey. When Trig comes back he works out a route for the birds so they have the best chance of making it to their planets.

A couple of birds are each packaged inside two small rockets. Each rocket will travel to a different planet. After the rocket enters a planet's atmosphere it will eject the hummers.

The hummer will then navigate around the planet and send back information about what it finds.

You put the rockets into launching tubes as Trig does some last minute checks of his calculations. Then you each hold a finger over a firing button.

"Four, three, two, one, launch!" says Trig.

As you press your button down you hear a thunderous sound from the hatches below.

The two of you race up to a viewing platform so you can see your robotic explorers departing. A twin set of lights move off into the distance and then separate as they head off to different worlds.

It might be that neither of the planets is suitable for living. They might have no water or no land or be too hot or too cold. Right now though, they are ripe with possibilities.

When you can't see their lights anymore Trig turns back to you,

"We'll have a few years to wait. Reckon we should go back to sleep?"

You hadn't thought about this but he's quite right. You are at the outskirts of a promising solar system but it will be a few years before the birds report back. You probably shouldn't waste time awake.

You sigh. No point in being too old to enjoy exploring a new planet. It's time to go back to sleep. It's frustrating though – being awake and running the space ship is exciting. You've never been in a position to do such important work. When you next wake you'll probably be a lowly servant to some rich passenger or working on a settler's farm to pay off your passage.

"Hey," says Trig, a note of cunning in his voice, "think you can re-program the robots to wake *us* up when the hummers report back?"

All the schematics for the *Victoria's* robots come into your mind. What a great education you got while you were asleep. If you could get the robots to wake you when the hummers report back, you will be able to have more adventures.

Trig watches you. The expression on his freckled face tells you he's trying to read your mind. He grins when he realizes you are thinking not about *if* you should do it but *how*.

Trig has gotten you into trouble before, though. It was his

suggestion to race the hummers that ended up with the ship going through a hole in space.

It is time to make a decision.

Do you agree to reprogram the ship to wake you? **P35**
Or
Do you let the ship decide who to wake? **P30**

Let the ship decide who to wake

The robotics repair shop is always busy. All day settlers come in with malfunctioning robots used to break in the new planet. There are machines that take down trees, machines that dig for coal and machines that defend the colony from the native animals.

You weren't woken when the *Victoria* first landed here several hundred years ago. Some passengers were kept asleep while others made the first explorations and discoveries. Some became rich securing land and resources, others are spoken of in legends. Since you were woken, you've worked on the huge robots and the little ones too. Sometimes you travel out on the steam railways into the country to work on immense machines that can't be brought in. Your employer is Mr. Wells, the great, great grandson of a woman who once captained the *Victoria* for a short time. You have seen a picture of her when you visited his house. Sometimes you dream about her and a red-headed boy. Is it a dream? It was long ago. You have a very busy life and you don't think about it much.

An old man comes in from the bright sunshine and squints into the shop. "Is anyone here?"

He's dressed like a rich farmer. You recognize him as the same fellow who came in a few months ago wanting to get an irrigation snake serviced. The snake came over on the space ship and was an exciting robot to work on. Its internal mechanism crunched through rock and soil and filtered out water which it converted to steam to power it.

"I'm here Mr. Bower," you say. "How can I help you?"

"Ah I was hoping I'd find you here, I know you like old bots." the old man says. "Take a look at this. We recently drained a small lake and found it with a metal detector. What do you think?"

He holds out a box. You take it to a work bench and carefully open it up. Inside is a dirty and dented little hummingbot.

"They had these flying about in the *Victoria*," you say as you gently clean away dirt. You're not too sure how you know this. The little bird is dented and faded but still has all its parts. You detach a little solar panel, clean away the dirt and find it surprisingly intact. You set the panel under a solar magnifier then you turn back to the hummer.

"We may not get her working again, but let's give it a try," you say. "These little bots are things of beauty. They had time for fine craftsmanship back then."

You open the main mechanism and look inside. There are a couple of rusted springs which you replace and then add some methane to the flying cartridge. Some of the clockwork has rusted out too and you carefully slot in new parts. You delicately file and polish each part so it fits perfectly. When you snap the bird back together it starts to move and then surprises you both by taking off around the room.

You head off to get a net to bring it down. It's a delicate old specimen and you don't want it falling and getting more damaged. To your surprise the little bird follows you.

"That's interesting," the old man says. "Did you ever get woken up when you traveled out on the *Victoria*?"

You try to think back. "I can't remember. I don't think so."

"This little fellow seems to know you. People often forget waking moments in space travel. You go back to sleep and learn new things. Without any triggers your brain buries memories quite deeply. You should find out – a lot of the records of that time were lost but if you helped get us here well… The descendants of folks who worked on board are claiming compensation these days. If you woke and helped get us here you could end up being rich enough to own this shop."

"But how would I ever prove something like that?" you ask.

The hummingbot emits a high-pitched whistle and attaches itself to an input on the computer you use to diagnose robot problems in remote areas. Before long, images start to play of corridors and 'sports racing inside the *Victoria*. The images change, now there is a close up of Captain Wells.

"That's my great grandmother!" exclaims a voice behind you.

It's your boss, back from a meeting. The three of you

keep watching. There's a scene where Captain Wells is in a padded room working on the controls. Something starts to tickle in your mind.

"This is amazing," Mr. Wells says, "this little hummingbot has footage of the famous moments when Captain Wells and a crew of two saved the entire ship after it was sucked through a black hole."

You keep watching. There are various scenes of the ship being fixed and then you see something extraordinary. A rocket is placed on the floor and the hummingbot moves towards it.

Two hands come up and take the little bird and it is placed inside. The robot looks upward as the rocket is sealed shut. The last image it shows is a face frowning in concentration.

It is your face.

"That's you!" your customer shouts. "It's really you. This is amazing."

Your life is about to change. As a hero from the original crews of the *Victoria* you'll be a celebrity and you'll also be entitled to land and riches.

The little bird gets down from the screen and flies over to you. You hold it in your hand. Now you remember sending it off on its journey.

"Thank you for coming back to me," you whisper to the little bird. It's like a piece of the puzzle of your life is back in place.

This part of your story has finished but things could have turned out quite differently. Would you like to:

Go back to the beginning of the story? **P1**

Or

Go to the List of Choices and start reading from another part of the story? **P172**

Agree to reprogram the ship to wake you

You and Trig speak to Captain Wells about your plan. She agrees that it's a good idea to program the robots to wake the three of you when the hummingbots return.

"We make a good team and I think we should be able to see where our actions have taken us. If you don't need any help, Trig and I will go check the rest of the cargo. We should make sure there aren't any problems after that big shake up the ship had."

You ask a hummer to show you the way to the main robotics chamber. The hummer takes you to an elevator which leads you down a couple of floors where you find a wide doorway with a smaller door set inside it. The door is specially designed so something large or small can pass through depending on the need at the time. The door isn't locked so you open the smaller door and step through into a large warehouse. Lights come on and illuminate everywhere you walk. Your footsteps echo on metal flooring. There are few human conveniences because the robots are programmed to undertake routine maintenance on themselves.

In one corner, a couple of spider bots sit near a collection of tools. A hummer flies in, its movement through the air a little erratic. You watch as the spider bots quickly replace its wing. Then one of them gently tosses the hummer into the air and it starts to fly again completely restored. The spider bots track the little hummer for a few moments to make sure it is fixed and then freeze to wait patiently for the next robot in need of fixing.

It's great to see this part of the ship working, but you also remember something you once heard in the orphanage when you were growing up – people used to do all the work before robots took over. When robots started doing everything, that's when some people couldn't afford to live honestly. You wonder why it had to be that way.

The middle of the room is taken up by high shelves with stores of robotic parts. You could make a vast variety of robots from them if you wanted – perhaps once on the new planet you will. More lights turn on and you gasp as you see a silent menagerie of different robots all along one wall. One is built like a giraffe, another like a snake. The snake is massively long and nearly the width of the ship's corridor. They must be here for some reason – the snake looks like it would be able to make big holes, perhaps the giraffe would make a good lookout if you were traveling through a forest.

Near the row of robots is a desk with what looks to be a link to the central console from which you can make changes to the ship's programming. You start up the console and are soon engrossed in the task of programming a wake-up instruction for yourself and the others.

"Excuse me. Could I ask why you are making changes to the ship's instructions?" a polite but non-human voice enquires.

You spin around to find that all the robots have moved closer to you. You nervously explain, sticking to the facts:

"Our team have found two planets in a new solar system and we're sending some hummers ahead to investigate. We need to sleep while we wait and we want the ship to wake us when there is more information."

You thought the idea was logical when Trig suggested it, but now you wonder if the robots will think you are overstepping your role. What will happen if they think you are not acting in the ship's best interests? There is quiet for a little while and then the giraffe's head turns toward you.

"We have decided that your change of protocol is acceptable. Please continue. We'll review the new program and if it is what you have told us, we will accept the new instructions."

You are relieved that the robots are happy with your plans and you continue to make the changes. When you finish you see the robots have silently moved back to where they were when you first came in.

"I'm finished now," you say, but nobody answers back. Apparently they have said all they needed to say. As you leave the chamber, the lights go out behind you.

Back with Trig and Captain Helena, you explain about the group of robots you saw. "I think they were guardians."

Captain Helena listens carefully to you. "We need to be careful about what we do – the ship is programmed to protect everyone and we're lucky it agreed with our decision.

We should get something to eat and enjoy a few hours of relaxation and then get to sleep."

She turns to a butler bot. "We'll take our meal in the hydroponic garden, thank you."

"Why do we want to go there?" you ask.

The Captain smiles, "You'll see."

You just hope she doesn't have you harvesting cabbages or something.

The butler heads off while the three of you run some final system checks.

Trig confirms the rockets are on track to make it to their respective planets. "It's all looking tickety-boo. They've covered thousands of miles already." He laughs. "We can wake up in a few years, look at the pictures they send back, and then decide to turn left or right."

The three of you race your 'sports down to the hydroponic gardens. The robotic control room was huge but the hydroponic chamber is even bigger. You expected some sort of garden factory so the beauty of the place surprises you.

You enter the garden through a little orchard of apple and pear trees so it's hard to see too far ahead. The fruit trees look deeply rooted and you wonder how far down the soil goes. It feels just like being outside on Earth. Springy moss carpets the ground. When you get out from between the fruit trees you see there are plants and vegetables everywhere. Vines run up the walls to high vaulted ceilings that remind you of a cathedral you once visited. Flying about through the garden are tiny butterfly robots that you suppose are used to pollinate the flowers. As you watch, a couple of hummingbots gently move a vine away from the lights that hang throughout the garden.

You walk to a small table sitting in a section of flower garden. The flowers don't seem to have any function except to be pretty. Captain Wells leans down and smells a rose and you do the same. The scent is heavenly.

Nearby you see a bushy shrub that has been trimmed into the shape of a large dog. It is so well done you can't see where the trunk is.

You are about to comment on the dog when a door opens in a far wall and a small car approaches you on a set of rails hidden in the dense moss. This miniature railway must be used to transport fruit and vegetables out of the garden.

Trig goes over and takes out a basket. He looks inside. "Lunch is served!"

"Or it could be dinner or breakfast," you say, "There's no day or night here, so we can't really say what sort of meal we're having."

"Whatever it is, it's a feast," Captain Wells declares, helping herself to baked potatoes.

You dive in too and soon you are all too busy eating to talk. In the quiet you hear a humming sound and realize there are some creatures in the garden with you - bees. As if to prove this, Trig pulls out a chunk of honeycomb from the basket and you all take a slice. It's deliciously sweet.

"That looks like fun," Trig says, pointing past the orchard where some strong vines are hanging from the ceiling. "Someone has woven them into swings."

"I think the seats are made from hemp," Helena says. "There's some growing over there. Hemp can be made into a fabric, like cotton. People used to use this to make clothes. Maybe they have a stock of it to make clothes for people once we arrive at a new planet."

Trig jumps on a swing and starts pumping his legs and leaning back. Before long his swing is covering a lot of ground. You both follow his lead and before long you are all soaring out over the garden – you can see a lot from here.

Out of the corner of your eye you catch some movement. It's very quick and when you look again you don't see anything.

"Someone must have had a bit of time awake to be making picnic tables and swings," Captain Wells says, keeping her voice deliberately calm but you think she's probably on the alert too.

"Are they still awake?" Trig asks, glancing around.

Maybe it was what Trig said but suddenly the gardens seem creepy and you feel a shudder run down your spine. Are you being watched? You stop swinging and jump off, signaling the other two to keep talking to cover your movement. You circle around to the place where you thought you saw movement, hoping to catch whoever it is unawares.

As you tiptoe past a large avocado tree you see a bent figure with gray hair hiding from behind another tree. Just as you are about to say something, you step on a twig. The sound startles the watcher and he jumps and whirls around to face you. He has a frightened look on his face.

"It's Okay, Sir," you say, "I'm not going to hurt you."

The man looks old compared to the three of you. "Oh dear," he says. "I didn't want you youngsters finding me. This is very awkward."

There is a rustle of leaves as Captain Wells appears through the greenery. She sees that the old man is fearful. "Sir, we were woken up to undertake a mission. We hope you fared well when the ship was carried through that hole in space recently. Are you alright?"

The Captain ignores the fact that there are people awake on the spaceship - who perhaps aren't supposed to be.

"A hole in space?" the man mutters. "So that's what caused all that rumpus. I was in the library with Eva. We were picking up books for hours."

You hear footsteps to your right. "Who is Eva?" Trig asks, causing the old man to startle once again.

"Oh nothing, nobody! Don't listen to me, I'm old and confused."

Clearly he's hiding something, but you don't think he means any harm.

"Did you make the swings?" you ask, hoping to shift him to an easier topic, "and the picnic table?"

"Yes. Did you enjoy them?"

Captain Wells nods. "Very much. We might have learned a lot from our time asleep, but we still love to play."

She leads the old man back to the picnic table and offers him tea. You join them looking around the chamber as they chat. You hadn't noticed the way some of the trees are shaped, or that there are decorative paths leading here and there, not to mention flowers and other plants and ornaments that just aren't essential at all. Someone has enjoyed living here.

"So," Captain Wells says, "I take it you were woken up at some stage and you didn't go back to sleep?"

"That's about it Captain."

The Captain sips her tea. "What did you wake up to do – topiary?"

"What's that?" Trig whispers to you.

The old man answers instead – it seems his hearing is perfectly alright. "Topiary is the art of shaping trees and bushes into interesting shapes young man." He pauses, "I'm sorry, I'm sure you're actually as old as I am, just better preserved."

You hadn't thought about age that way. But before you have a chance to comment the old man continues.

"I was woken up to take care of some issues here in the hydroponic garden – the bees were dying. I woke and found

I knew about bees and plants and even the art of cultivating new hybrids."

"And after a while you were too old to go back to sleep?" asks the Captain.

"This is a pretty good life – I have a beautiful garden and all the fruit and vegetables I can eat. There is a wonderful library down the corridor and I'm always able to look at the stars. I'm sorry, I haven't introduced myself, my name is Amos."

As the Captain introduces the three of you and explains a bit about your mission, you notice one of the topiary bushes has changed its shape. Or are you imagining it? You're sure it was a dog shape, now it looks more like a rabbit. Or is it just the angle? You wander away from the others, aiming to look at the bush from another direction. Maybe you're confused and there is a dog somewhere else.

You jump on a swing and pump your legs to gain some height. You gaze over the rest of the garden. From above you see quite a few topiary bushes. There's one shaped like a lion and another like an elephant and there are sheep and other animals you don't know the names of. As you watch you notice something else – they are moving!

Three small rabbit-shaped bushes roll together and form a ball and from that appears the shape of a big cat. A lioness. It paces forward without a need for roots and it heads for Trig and the Captain.

You jump off the swing and run back toward them, but

you're blocked by a green wall of leaves and twigs growing up in front of you!

You dodge off to the left, and a ball of green speeds ahead and reforms into another wall. You try and force your way through instead.

At first you think you've outsmarted the plant when you feel the wall give way, but then the plant closes around you and you lose your balance as you're rolled up inside a new ball. You've been snared by a monster plant.

Just as you're thinking you might throw up that picnic lunch you had earlier, the rolling ball of leaves comes to a stop. You're leaning a bit to one side, but it could be worse, you could be upside down. You can see through the branches that you're facing two other balls and the old man. You can just make out Trig and the Captain staring out of plant balls that encase them too.

"Alright Eva, let our guests sit down," says the old man. The foliage around you reforms to make a chair. You notice however that you seem to have some sort of vine seatbelt on.

"You owe us an explanation," the Captain says from her chair. "Your plant is currently undertaking an act of mutiny. I want an explanation!"

She still talks as if she is in charge even when she's strapped into a living plant.

Trig is looking at her with complete faith that she'll get you out of this – he's changed since you first met, when he couldn't believe a girl could be in charge of the ship.

The old man starts talking:

"Many years ago, I was woken to help with problems in the ship's garden with the bees. The plants were only just surviving. While I was sleeping I'd learned a lot about modern gardening techniques but I knew we needed new methods in space. I also knew that gardens need a gardener – this place is huge but it's too small to rely on robot monitoring. Some things really do need a human touch. I woke up a scientist and we experimented to develop plants that didn't need as much of a root system and other plants that could tell us about what was wrong with the garden. All of the plants here are hybrids of what was originally stocked on the *Victoria* – all except Eva here – she's very special: a combination of human and plant genetics. A whole new species."

"Where's the other scientist you worked with?" Trig asks.

"Sleeping," says the old man. "We worked together for a number of years and then decided someone needed to stay awake with Eva and one of us should sleep. Eva will live a long time. She's very special, adaptable and intelligent. She's our baby – we want her to have a great life. When I'm near the end of my days I'll wake Eva's mother and sister and they can decide what to do next with her."

"Eva has a sister?" you say. You imagine a plant sleeping in a sleep pod.

"Her sister is human – like us. We decided to stay awake

for a few years to see Eva settled into the garden. During that time we also had her sister, Esmeralda. When she turned twelve we decided it would be a good idea if Esmeralda went to sleep like everyone else so that she could live to see a new planet. My partner went to sleep beside her so that she will have her mother when she wakes. That was fifty five years ago."

Trig sighs, completely captivated by the story. "So you said goodbye to the woman you love so you could stay with one of your kids?"

Captain Wells isn't quite so fascinated by the romance of the story. "But the real question is, do we still need Eva to keep the hydroponic garden here working well?"

"No, she's managed to get it optimized. Her purpose is fulfilled."

"Hmm so if I've followed you correctly, you've created a plant that is intelligent and can make changes in an environment that will improve the chances of other plants growth?"

"That's right Captain, Eva would have been a great boon on Earth. She could have brought new life to places we'd destroyed with mining and pollution. You've seen what she can do – she can make herself into many plants or merge into one. She's very adaptive."

"Have you ever thought about Eva's potential to make a whole planet more habitable?"

The old man stared at her, his mind ticking over. "Well

it's possible - there would need to be water and carbon dioxide – that's what she needs. And some heat. But Eva doesn't need the same conditions humans do."

"That's what I thought," Captain Wells says. "But awake here on her own she's a bit of a liability, and you, Amos, are in limbo unable to sleep for fear of what her 'adaptations' might do unchecked?"

Amos nods his head slowly as the Captain continues.

"We've just sent a couple of probes to two planets ahead of us. The ship will take a lot longer to get there and there are several other planets that don't have all the right conditions for us – but if Eva got there first she could make a closer planet ready for humans."

"I see what you mean!" The old man brightens, but then looks doubtful. "Well, it would be up to Eva naturally."

"Does she understand what we're saying?" asks Trig.

You are pretty sure the plant *does* understand everything that's being said. If Captain Wells doesn't come up with a good plan for Eva you suspect you could become fertilizer for this garden. Eva, like all other living things, will fight for her survival.

You need to help. "Captain," you say, "Permission to look at equipping a shuttle for Eva to make a journey between the stars."

"Permission granted," says the Captain, then she calmly speaks to the plant holding you all. "Eva, let my engineer and the navigator out of the garden so they can see about finding you a better home."

Has Eva been following your conversation? Is she going to let you go?

You try and relax. If the plant picks up on emotions, your racing heart will let her know that you don't entirely trust her. In fact you've been wondering if the ship is carrying any chemicals to make a giant dose of weed killer. There's no way Amos could have left her alone on the ship. She's not like a robot, just following a program. She thinks for herself, and she might come up with something the people on the ship wouldn't like.

The vines and branches wrapping you onto the chair loosen; the cushion pushes you upward to a standing position.

Eva seems to be in agreement with the plan. You walk toward the door with Trig beside you. You look back and find the Captain still seated – Eva hasn't let her go. Next to you, a little green doglike creature pads along. It seems like Eva is going to tag along. You wonder how well this little dog can communicate back to the main plant.

The Captain continues to act as if she's in control of the situation. "Go and investigate potential planets for Eva. It needs to be a place where we can be sure she'll survive and where her family can join her. Her job will be to prepare their new home. I'll stay here a while longer and make some preparations with Amos."

Outside the hydroponic garden you and Trig jump on

transporters. The green dog paces alongside you when you take off. From time to time it forms a ball and rolls along before changing dog form again. You can't help thinking it would make a great pet.

Back on the bridge, Trig searches through nearby planetary systems he'd discounted earlier. You stare at the schematics for the various small shuttles on the *Victoria* and think about how they could be adapted to accommodate Eva.

Your work takes hours and twice a robot comes in with a small meal. There is still no signal from the Captain and you assume Eva still holds her captive.

"This is an interesting one," Trig says at last.

The green dog has been lying on the floor as if asleep but it gets up and trots over with you to look at what Trig has found.

You lean over Trig's shoulder and look at the planet he is pointing out. The green dog's tail coils up the desk and the rest of it unravels like a long strand of ivy. Once it has spooled onto the top of the desk it becomes a dog shape again.

"Excellent trick, Eva," you say. The green dog wags its tail then taps with its paw on the map. Trig tells you about what he's found.

"This is a volcanic planet with mountains of glass-like rock that form most of its land mass. There are also some plains and a big ocean. I discounted it earlier because the mountains looked uninhabitable, but Eva should be able to create adaptations that would make it quite pleasant. What do you think, Eva?"

The little dog looks at the information on the screen and seems to be reading.

You recall Amos talking about picking up the books in the library so perhaps Eva can read. After a while the dog wags its tail and jumps off the desk and runs to the door. It looks back at you both, clearly telling you that it's time to go back to Amos and the Captain.

On the way back to the garden you have a sudden inspiration and stop your transporter. "I need to go and look at something – now I know what sort of planet Eva's going to, there might be something that will be really helpful. I just have to ask the robots if it's okay to use it."

You head back to the programming room. As before, all the robots are quiet.

You sit down and start talking but can't tell if they are listening or not. You explain about Eva – about how the plant is so special but can't really be left on its own while everyone sleeps. You explain about the glass mountain planet and how Eva might make it a special place to live.

After you've finished your explanations, the giraffe takes a step forward and speaks. "Your logic is sound. You can take the supplies you want but with one condition. You must send 100 sleepers – male and female – along with Eva. Our trip is long and dangerous, we may not find an optimal planet for our cargo. It is logical to send some to this planet as a backup settlement in case ours is destroyed."

The giraffe-bot stops speaking and steps back. Its companion stirs. It fills the hallway perfectly as it follows you to the garden.

When you get there you find Trig, Amos, and Captain Wells talking excitedly about the new planet. It appears Eva is keen to go. But there is stunned silence when the giant snake robot slithers into the garden.

"What's that for?" asks Amos.

"For making tunnels in the glass mountains. They'll be shelter and more. The ship has agreed to send it with Eva to help prepare for your family and 97 others."

Amos looks confused. "Others?"

You explain what the ship has decided, about investing 100 passengers on settling the planet.

"Then I guess we just need to decide something for ourselves," says Captain Wells.

"What's that?" says Trig.

"We need to decide if we get off at Glass Mountain or carry on."

Trig looks at you, suddenly excited – "I bet you could invent some great devices to slide down those mountains."

"And we'd own land and be our own bosses," you say.

He's right, the planet has all sorts of potential. Still, this will be a tough decision: There are many risks in putting so much hope on the abilities of a plant.

It is time to make a decision.

Do you want to risk a less than perfect planet and go with Eva? **P56**

Or

Leave Eva and continue on between the stars? **P53**

Leaving Eva

The next few weeks are busy. You and the others are waking people and briefing them about the landing. There are three ships to get ready, including one with the huge mining snake. Eva makes herself very useful during the preparations, in particular, deciding on seeds and livestock to take to the new planet. On the third day you go with Amos and Eva's little dog to wake up Amos' daughter Esmeralda and her mother. There is a tearful reunion of the whole family. Esmeralda asks if her father might be able to take a sleep pod or two to the new planet. She thinks it might be nice for him to sleep for a few years while they set up their new home. Amos isn't too sure he wants to miss more time with his family but they agree the pods might come in useful.

Everywhere Esmeralda goes a little green dog pads after her – the two are inseparable. Some of the other passengers are a little bit wary of Eva. Eva senses this and tries to devise ways to get the settlers to know and trust her.

She splits herself up into lots of green balls that follow the settlers about. It becomes natural for the settlers to use their 'tumble weeds' as chairs and cushions. Before long people are very comfortable with Eva and you think that the ship will be missing a great asset when the landing parties have gone.

The day comes when the little ships are loaded and

launched into space. Each passenger rests against a green pillow soaked in natural herbs cultivated by Amos. Where once the settlers might have felt frightened or anxious, the pillow has a soothing effect.

"It smells like lavender," says one traveler.

"Mine smells like the old roses my grandmother used to grow," says another.

You watch from the bridge as the three ships leave the *Victoria* and head to the planet. Each of these vessels will make a temporary shelter for the settlers until the snake makes tunnels and caves for them to live in. They will not all land together as you don't want them to accidentally crash. Instead Trig has set them on courses to land on different parts of the planet. One will land in the mountains and another on the plains. They have plenty of equipment to build a new Britannia.

When the settlers have gone there is no more reason to stay awake. After a last meal you take a final tour of the *Victoria* on your transporters. You still haven't even been through half of it. A little hummingbot follows you through corridors. Behind you both, a small green ball rolls along as though attached by an invisible thread.

You know you shouldn't put it off much longer. It's time to head to your sleep pod and immerse yourself in warm jelly. You look forward to the sleeping cap teaching you wonderful new things. Just as you lose consciousness you look out through the glass. You must be dreaming already, for a moment you thought you saw a little green dog wagging its tail and chasing a green ball…

You have finished this part of your story. It is time for another decision. Would you like to:

Go back to the beginning and try another path? **P1**

Or

Go to the List of Choices and start reading from another part of the story? **P172**

On Eva's planet

Three landing ships set off from the *Victoria* to the glass planet. A part of Eva traveled on each ship.

The largest ship carried the robot snake. It was used by the settlers to make tunnels into the mountains. Eva adapted a local fungus to be highly nutritious. It could be grown hydroponically within these caverns. Over time the settlers adapted to mountain living. They discovered diamonds and used them for grip while traveling over the smooth glass surface.

The snake robot didn't get on with the new native fungus and burrowed deeper and deeper into the mountains. It returned to the highlands less and less often and eventually stopped coming altogether. But by then it had done its job and the settlements were well established.

The second ship landed on the plains so the settlers started farming. There were many native plants and species which helped them have a good life. Sometimes these settlers glanced up at the mountains and wondered why anyone would want to make their homes there.

The plains dwellers, or Lowlanders as they became known, were often visited by the inhabitants of the third ship who explored the rest of the planet and developed a roving nature. Over time, members of this third group became traders – delivering goods and news between the different communities.

After a few hundred years with no written history, people forgot entirely where they came from. There were rumors that they had come from the stars and stories about metal creatures which dug tunnels and robots that did other useful things abounded. But nobody knew for sure. Many thought the stories were only legend.

Sometimes a Highlander would take it into their head to develop new machines and start drilling and banging and thinking. They'd eat a bit of fungus and things would become clearer and their inventions more ingenious.

While the Highlanders were inventing machines, the Lowlanders enjoyed the many green tumbleweeds they found rolling around the planet (and which were so convenient as cushions and pillows). Settlers would snuggle into a tumble weed and before they knew it – more tumble weed would attach to the first and a cozy bed would form. Naps were common.

Other tumble weeds would roll off to make themselves useful as baby's cribs or settle under a roof being fixed in case a worker fell off.

People used to say. "It's like those tumbleweeds know what's going on."

The End

Psst! you can read more about the planet Eva went to when you read *Secrets of Glass Mountain*, but for now you might want to explore some more of *Between the Stars*:

Would you like to:

Go back to the beginning and try another path? **P1**

Or

Go to the list of choices and start reading from another part of the book? **P172**

The mission

"Are you crazy Trig?"

You can't believe he wants to play with the equipment. "Let's get this radiation problem sorted."

"Nobody else is awake," says Trig, "We're in charge. Besides, we might get there faster."

You point to a floor plan of the spaceship attached to a nearby wall. "Look, there's an equipment room not far ahead. That's where we need to go."

You set off on your transporter and Trig paces next to you, looking disappointed, so you cheer him up.

"Last one there's a rotten egg," you yell.

Trig lets out a whoop, opens up his transporter, and surges ahead. You chuckle as he speeds right past the room and you get there first anyway.

The place is a treasure trove. Gathering things to equip the spider-bot is easy because things are so well organized. You pick up tools you never knew about back on Earth and confidently assess them. It's astonishing what you've learned.

When Trig joins you he calls a hummingbot over and starts to make adaptations to the little bird. After Trig's changes, the hummingbots fly up to a methane tank one by one and suck up gas through their 'beaks'. Their wings won't work in the same way in space, they will need jet propulsion. As they take in the gas they change color to an iridescent blue.

You peer at a hummingbot's delicate metallic head. "If the Captain wants to see more, we need to give the hummers better optics."

You fit the hummingbot with a new eye piece, rather like a monocle. The robotic bird tries to fly but the extra weight is too much. You know that won't be a problem outside the ship though. In space it will be weightless. You add a little device that gives it a perch on the spider-bot.

"Nice," says Trig. "With that perch it can leave and re-enter the ship without flying at all."

Trig tucks the now flightless hummingbot into the pannier on his transport. Side by side you race to the airlock and set up the birds and spider-bot ready for their excursion.

The little hummers retract their wings and lie in a circle around the spider bot, while the one with the special long distance scope sits on its perch.

When the airlock opens, the birds will fire their jets and fly outside. Then, in formation, they will start their inspection.

The spider-bot will clamber outside, holding tight to the ship's hull, and go where you direct it from your console in the control room.

You and Trig step out of the airlock and close the hatch behind you. Once on the other side, you wind the mechanism that opens the outside hatch to let the bots out.

You watch the hummingbots float out and the spider,

using its suction feet, walk out carrying the last bird, then head back to the bridge on your 'sports to follow them remotely and direct the repairs. You don't want to waste any time, so you both release all the power you stored on the ride down. The speed and low gravity mean you can hold on to the handle bars and let your body streak out behind you.

Trig is riding along beside you and you grin at each other as you race along. Abruptly Trig drops back and you look ahead just in time to avoid Captain Wells who is standing at the door of the bridge.

"That looks like so much fun," she says wistfully. "Come into the control room and let's get these repairs finished. We can all go for a race once the work is done."

You are relieved at the Captain's reaction. It seems bad to be enjoying the ride so much when the ship is in danger, but you couldn't help yourself.

At the console Trig starts monitoring the hummingbots. He's checking their flight plans and making little adjustments. "So far so good – there's a chance of collision so I'm mapping their progress. We should start getting some pictures about… now."

The monitor splits into several windows at once. The hummingbot with the high-powered telescope detaches from the spider bot and blasts away from the ship to start mapping this sector of deep space.

You are seeing the stars from a perspective no human eyes have ever seen before. "Wow look at all those galaxies!"

The hummingbots are starting their ship scan. You watch the golden-bronze exterior of the ship as they cover every inch. There are large circular port holes with their irises tightly shut to streamline the ship and protect it from meteors and heat loss.

A few portholes are open to allow light to filter into the hydroponic gardens. These gardens make oxygen for the ship and nutrients for the sleepers. Waste from the sleepers is recycled back to the garden. You know that this system loses energy slowly and that the ship can't travel forever, but by gathering solar heat from the stars you pass, the gardens can last a long time. But everything wears out eventually. And you know that in time, the gardens won't be able to function. You'll need to have found a new planet by then.

As you survey, another porthole you see it twitching – not quite shutting completely. It's jammed up somehow. This will be part of the reason the ship has been using more power than normal. It needs to be fixed before the ship can enter a new planet's atmosphere. The heat on entering a planet's atmosphere is tremendous. All the portholes must be closed for the space ship to land safely.

You signal to Trig and he gets a hummingbot to move closer to see what is happening. The surface of the ship isn't smooth – it is covered in several layers of metal feathers. As the hummingbot zooms in on the outside of the ship, you start to see some odd looking space debris clinging to the hull and coating the iris of the malfunctioning porthole.

"That's odd," says Trig, "Looks like a large cloud of some sort of dust has hit us. Maybe it's space poo."

"Space poo?" you say. "Is that a technical term?"

Trig blushes and looks at the Captain, but she's absorbed in what you are seeing on the screen and doesn't react.

"Let's get a sample," you say. "We're going to need to get that iris cleaned up so the porthole can close again before we enter a new atmosphere or we could roast the ship."

Trig directs one of the hummingbots to collect samples of dust as the spider bot starts cleaning the debris off the outside of the ship. The dust all moves in one direction as if there's a breeze out there. You wonder what could be causing it to move one way.

You keep watching the feeds that show the debris cleaning operation, making adjustments to the spider's progress.

The Captain taps her monitor. "There's an awful lot of nothing showing in the starboard quadrant. Is my screen broken or is something strange going on?"

The special hummingbot has been feeding back a steady view of the stars, but when you look at what it is relaying now, you see only a vast blackness. As you watch, the trail of dust the spider-bot has disturbed moves into the blackness and disappears. "Something in the darkness is drawing it in," you say.

"Is it getting bigger, or are we getting closer?" asks the Captain, a touch of nerves showing in her voice.

Trig gets busy with his controls and looks up with a white face.

"We're drifting towards it Captain." Then Trig turns to you. "How much longer do you need? I don't want to get any closer to this thing whatever it is."

You check the bots. Thankfully they are nearly finished. You signal the spider-bot to get clear of the port hole and watch with satisfaction as the iris shuts smoothly. The hummingbots transmit images of a gleaming set of feathers all over the ship – the debris has been removed. You want to check the sample to see what that dust is made of so you order the bots to come back inside.

"Can you get the hummer to take a wider view of that empty patch, Trig?" The Captain says, obviously intrigued by the nothingness.

But before Trig has a chance to do anything, the little hummer has turned its scope toward the place with no stars. It breaks away from its orbit of the ship and starts drifting faster and faster out into space towards the darkness.

"Can you get it back Trig?" asks the Captain.

Trig tries to bring the hummer back but then shakes his head. "It's no good. Gravitational pull is too strong."

The three of you watch the little bird from the more limited scope of one of the other little hummers which Trig has turned to follow it's lost colleague's path.

You know the little robot isn't alive but you still feel sad as it disappears, knowing it hasn't a chance of getting back inside the ship.

"Speed it up crew, we need to get moving," says the Captain calmly. "Or we're the ones that will be space poo."

Once the bots are back inside, you switch off your monitor and head towards the door. "I'm going to analyze that dust."

The Captain nods as she works to reset the *Victoria's* course.

Then Trig pipes up, "The magnetic field is back at almost 100 percent."

Pleased that the problem has been fixed, you step outside and take a 'sport down to a lab room. The spider-bot is waiting for you when you arrive. The sample turns out to be almost pure platinum. No wonder the dust was interfering with the artificial polarity in the center of the ship. But how did it get there? Was it some sort of freak event? More importantly, is it likely to happen again?

The spider-bot follows you back to the bridge. When it falls behind, you put it on the 'sport and give it a ride.

"You were carrying a fortune, little spider," you tell it. "Platinum is even rarer than gold."

On a whim you stop at a storage room and find some room on a shelf. You write your name and number on a slip of paper and put it, and most of the platinum, in an empty box. Who knows, if you ever find yourself on a planet, that dust might be worth something.

One of the hummingbots flies along beside you – perhaps

it has some relationship to the spider-bot, it seems to keep a constant distance from it. Maybe Trig programmed it to stay close and hadn't thought about changing the instructions once the hummer was back inside the ship.

You come to a fork in the corridor. The way to the Captain's quarters is smooth metal inlaid with the magnetic strips that stabilizes butlers and other bots that roam the ship, but to your right the corridor is carpeted in a deep green moss. You haven't seen anything like it elsewhere on the ship. You make a mental note to report this unexpected growth to Captain Wells.

The Captain smiles when you enter. Trig gives you a thumbs up.

"Now that the magnetic field is back to normal we've increased speed and moved away from that blackness," Trig says.

"But what caused the dust?" the Captain asks. "We can't go back to sleep and leave this unexplained."

"I think I know why the electromagnetic field was compromised," you say, as you take out the small sample of platinum powder.

"The precious metal interfered with the magnetic core of the ship and reduced the ship's artificial magnetic field and therefore its ability to withstand radiation," you say. "But I don't know where the platinum dust came from."

The spider-bot and the hummingbot move to a console and appear to be communicating with the ships main computer. The Captain inspects what they are up to and alerts you that the ship is taking evasive action to avoid a meteor shower.

"The *Victoria's* been instructed to move away from meteors so we don't take any damage. Strap yourselves in, we'll be…"

She doesn't have time to say any more. The ship lurches as it accelerates and swerves. Then once it's cleared the meteors it resumes a smooth quiet path through space.

"Let's see what we avoided," says Trig. He opens one of the viewing portals and magnifies the view. You look at the herd of meteors moving through space and wonder what explosion propelled them in your direction.

"What's that?" says Trig, wiggling dials to magnify a glinting speck tucked amongst the cluster of space rocks. As Trig zooms in, the speck grows larger.

You're amazed he even noticed it. "You've got sharp eyes."

When Trig goes on to full zoom, you see another spaceship, and it appears to be heading *towards* the meteor shower you just avoided. You are fascinated as the other ship draws a large boulder out of the whirling mass of space rocks with some kind of tractor beam.

"It's separating that one from the pack," says Captain Wells. "You've got to admire how they maneuver through those meteors without getting hit."

"They're a lot smaller than us," Trig points out.

"And nimbler too," muses the Captain.

The captured meteor glows and then contracts. In no time the meteor crumples like a wad of paper. Part of the once giant rock is sucked into the spaceship and the rest drifts away, pulverized to microscopic particles.

"I think we know what caused our dust," Trig announces. "But why would they dump such a precious metal? It doesn't make sense."

"What would you do with precious metals out here? What could be more precious than that to them?" asks the Captain.

"Water!" you say. "It makes a crazy sort of sense. Everything contains a small amount of water, even rocks."

"Must take a lot of power to crumple a meteor just for a few buckets of water," muses the Captain. "I could see the value in capturing icy comets, but rock. They must be desperate?"

You and Trig look at each other, thinking the same thing.

Trig speaks it out loud, "Would they do the same thing to us?"

"Hopefully not," says Captain Wells, "Still, I think it would be a good idea to get some more distance between the *Victoria* and that ship. We want to avoid getting another dust shower."

You consider what the Captain has said. If that ship was responsible for our first dusting, it had the opportunity to treat the *Victoria* like that meteorite before you were woken up. But it didn't. The strange space ship can't be an enemy. You explain your theory to the Captain and she agrees, but still thinks she should be cautious. You agree to use some reserve power and move out of the area.

That sorted, the Captain rubs her belly. "Let's have lunch. I might not know what that ship is doing out there, but I do know I haven't had a proper meal in 170 years."

A butler-bot appears and folds down a dining table from a wall. Dining chairs are set up and vegetables and a freshly roasted chicken are delivered to the table. There is a wine bottle and three elegant glasses. Trig picks up the bottle.

"Elderflower cordial – not what I was hoping for but I'm sure it's a great drop." He fills everyone's glass.

You all start eating. Your stomach growls as you savor your first mouthful.

The Captain puts down her fork. "While you were readying the bots I read through some of the messages the ship has received. Things have changed on Earth. More ships have been sent out, including mining ships. There are space stations reaching out across the universe and there are other peoples living in space.

"There were several messages for the *Victoria* asking if she'd found a new home. One informed us that the planets we were heading towards might be occupied before we get to them."

"How could that be?" Trig asks.

"Newer technology. Other ships have passed us even

though they left after we did. That craft we saw harvesting the meteor could be one of those ships. There's no record of us being hailed though."

"Maybe we should try and communicate with it?" Trig suggests. "Maybe it can send us in the right direction."

"I don't like the look of that ship," says the Captain. "We were woken to deal with a technical problem and we've sorted it. If we're going to engage with that ship I think we need to change staff – we aren't diplomats and negotiators. If we make contact we need to wake people better suited to the task and go back to sleep ourselves."

You need to make a decision. Do you:

Get a new crew on the job and go back to sleep? **P115**

Or

Avoid the other ship? **P71**

You have chosen to avoid the other ship

Trig sets a course away from the mining ship. You are now running at full power, having fixed the problems you were woken up to sort out.

"We'll stay awake for a few more days so we can monitor that ship," says Captain Wells.

With the autopilot on and no more urgent tasks at hand, you all set about exploring the ship. You start by checking out the sleeping animals and wonder what species have been stocked on board. Perhaps the ship is like a Noah's ark in space.

Trig offers to help the Captain get through the news and messages. You're surprised about this, you thought he'd be off riding around on the 'sports to see how fast he could get them going.

You ask a hummingbot to guide you down into the livestock compartment.

The livestock bay holds horses and cattle and sheep and even birds in special sleep tanks, each engineered especially for them. There are dogs and pigs too. You wander around looking at the animals as they move in their sleep. In another area you find monkeys sleeping. They seem to have similar sleeping apparatus to your own. Are they learning too?

"What are the monkeys learning?" you ask the hummer.

The hummer flies over to a set of files on a shelf. You

remember learning that it is important to stimulate the brain while sleeping. You expect that the material is geared specifically to animals, perhaps the monkeys are dreaming of bananas. You chuckle. The dogs are receiving instruction too, and the horses. Several tanks at the back of the room are empty. They look like the one you slept in.

"Can I help you?" asks a voice.

A young man steps out of the shadows, he looks at you with his head tilted to one side.

"Hello," you say, and explain that you were exploring the ship while you wait for the next part of your mission.

"Know much about space sleeping do you?" asks the man. It's hard to tell if he's annoyed about your intrusion or not.

"I don't think so, Sir," you say. "I know something about robotics, and the engineering of the ship. That was why I was woken up. I didn't see much of the ship before I went to sleep so I just thought I'd look around. I hope you don't mind?"

"I'm naturally a little cautious," says the man. "You can call me Dr Ralph if you like. I take it you were a convict sentenced to transportation?"

"That's right, Dr Ralph, sir."

"What was the nature of your crime?"

You think back to that moment that seems only weeks ago but really it's whole lifetimes ago.

"I stole food Dr Ralph. Quite a lot of it."

"Tell me more."

You walk around the livestock compartment again, telling Dr Ralph about growing up in the orphanage and never knowing your parents. How you'd been apprenticed to a baker before your tenth birthday and worked long hours. You tell him about all the hungry people in the streets, including a few you grew up with in the orphanage. Over time, you worked out ways to siphon out stale bread to give to them. It wasn't much but you didn't think you were hurting anyone.

"Those poor people should have signed up for the factories," Dr Ralph mused.

"People don't come back from there," you tell him.

A serious look crosses his face. "There are many, I believe, that make a better life and don't need to return but, I agree, there are tales of wrongdoing in the far reaches of Britannia."

"It is not easy to hire out your labor when there are robots who can work longer hours and make less mistakes. The cities of Londoninium were flooded with unemployed. That's why men like us decided on the transportation initiative. Unskilled people like yourselves can become highly skilled people while you sleep and we can build a better society in a land where there is room for us all."

Dr Ralph seems to have lost his distrust in you, although he isn't treating you as an equal like Captain Wells seems to do. You wonder how different a new society will be if people like him still think they are more important than commoners like you.

"Tell me," he says, changing tack, "have you ever played draughts or chess?"

"Yes Sir, and card games too," you tell him.

"Excellent!" He declares. "Desmond – step out and meet a new friend."

A huge monkey swings down from some pipes running along the high ceiling. When you look up you see several monkeys of different types up there. They must have been watching you ever since you came into the room.

"Desmond here is a chimpanzee," says Dr Ralph. "He's part of a breeding program started by my great-grandfather who pioneered the sleep method we use for space travel. "Desmond loves games of all sorts."

"Hello Desmond," you say, looking at the ape.

Desmond is almost as tall as you are and looks strong. The chimpanzee leans forward to sniff you. You doubt he's met many people before.

Desmond gestures for you to join him at a table and shows you various games. You start with snakes and ladders and then move on to something more complicated. You are surprised at how good Desmond is at chess, but he takes a long time to move, and enjoys swinging around from various pipes and brackets while he thinks about it.

Dr Ralph explains that his experimental program to improve the thinking abilities of animals was overlooked at the universities on Earth because everyone was interested in robotics. "Animals have only ever been interesting to men if they can eat them or get them to work," he says bitterly.

You can see he is passionate about his work and why he was so wary about you. Something puzzles you though. How long has Dr Ralph been awake?

"Dr Ralph I understand I've been asleep for nearly two hundred years. You seem to be one of the oldest people I've met on the ship but you can't have been asleep all this time?"

"You've caught me on one of my waking cycles," explains the scientist. "I didn't know how the animals would fare with the sleep jelly so I volunteered to wake every hundred years or so and run some tests. The animals have done well. I've made some adaptations to our research program. I've got them all learning as they sleep now. They will be even more useful when we get to a new planet."

Two more apes come down from the ceiling and start playing cards. Desmond beats you at chess and then brings out a game you haven't seen before. Patiently, he shows you the pieces as he pulls them out of a wooden box. There are hand carved animals and an intricate set of three boards that connect on rods. You see that the boards represent land, sea and sky. The game is beautiful and complex.

Each creature has a unique way of moving and each creature has both an enemy and a friend. Ingenious.

"Is this something the aristocrats play?" you ask.

Dr Ralph shakes his head. "It's a game the animals have devised."

The animals look at you expectantly. One of the chimps raises his eyebrows, tilts his head to one side and leans slightly forward.

"It's a fabulous game," you say. As you settle down to learn the rules, you help yourself to fruit that one of the monkeys brings around.

You take the role of a zebra and team up with a baboon to find water and food and escape a flood and a fire and an attack by lions. Eventually, you have to make a choice: join a herd or, if you want to, you can keep on with your baboon friend and a snake you've teamed up with.

As the game progresses, you wonder how things might have turned out if you'd made different alliances.

After a couple hours of game playing, you feel really tired and tell Desmond and the Doctor that you need some sleep. "Maybe there will be better treatment of animals on our new planet?"

Dr Ralph shrugs. "I'm not too hopeful. The rest of the cargo is filled with robots and new steam creations. We're just a backup."

On the next level you run into Trig and the Captain and ask them where your sleeping quarters might be. They take you to a section of the ship for passengers who are awake. There are just a few other people about, some are quite old.

"These are people who chose not to go back to sleep,"

whispers Trig. "They have jobs mostly in the hydroponic gardens. I spoke to a few of them earlier. I'm thinking about staying awake too."

"Welcome, travelers," says one of the men. "We hear you successfully sorted our engineering problem earlier. Thank you so much. You must be tired."

He shows you to a bunk room. It is big enough to sleep several people, but right now there is just you. There is no day or night in space so you figure people just set up their own sleep rhythms.

There's a spare set of clothing laid out at the foot of the bed and some snacks on a shelf nearby. Despite being bone tired you find it hard to go to sleep – you haven't slept in a bed for years and it all feels a bit odd. You lie there thinking about the events of the last hours. So much has happened and your life is so incredibly different to the one you had on planet Earth. You think about Trig wanting to stay awake and wonder if you should stay awake too? Space is very big and there may be no more excitement until you all reach a new planet. Would you want to miss that? Life is full of decisions; it would be so good if you could see how different choices played out. Eventually you nod off.

You wake with a feeling that you aren't alone in the bunk room. When you open your eyes you find Trig and Desmond quietly playing a game of cards.

"Someone taught this monkey how to play Wild Ladies," Trig says, when he notices you stirring. "I came in here to wake you up and he's sitting on the end of your bed telling me to be quiet. Next thing I know he brings out a deck of cards and I thought he might do something bad if I didn't play along. Turns out he's a proper card shark."

"He's good at all sorts of games," you say.

"You know him then?"

"Yeah, we met yesterday. I didn't know he was allowed to roam around the spaceship though. Where's Dr Ralph, Desmond?"

Desmond looks at you and mimes sleeping. Then he points to a large bag.

"What's inside Desmond?" The chimp passes you the bag. "It's his animal game," you tell Trig. "This is excellent. Let's get some breakfast and play it."

When you sit down to a meal, Desmond sits with you. None of people who are awake seem surprised to see him so you figure he must be fairly well known.

You clear the table and are about to set up the game when the Captain comes in.

"We might have trouble," she says. Then she stops and looks at Desmond. "What's with the monkey?"

"He's a chimpanzee," you say. "What's up?"

"That spaceship is following us. The one that crunches meteorites. The holiday is over."

"Sorry Desmond," you say. "Duty calls."

Back at the bridge, you're not really sure what help you'll be – this isn't an engineering problem.

Captain Wells starts pulling up information. "I didn't want to worry you before, but I know something about the ship that's following us. Apparently it's run by a Chinese pirate called Ching Shee."

"A pirate!" Trig exclaims. He comes over to look at the dispatches.

"These are messages we've been sent since we left – there isn't much. Earth stopped transmitting to us more than one hundred years ago.

"Not long after we left, the Chinese Emperor sent some spaceships out too. The idea was to find new land just like Britannia. They had a terrible problem of overpopulation, just like us. The Emperor commissioned his best ship builders but a notorious pirate commandeered the space ship factory and sent out several ships herself.

"The pirate is called Ching Shee and her builders appear to have improved the technology the Chinese had originally. Our own science was kept a strict secret. They don't have our sleeping caps and sleep jelly for instance."

Trig interrupts: "Then Ching Shee must be long dead. Someone else must be commanding the ship."

Captain Wells shakes her head. "I said they didn't have sleep jelly, but they do have something else to manage years of space flight. Cloning."

"What do you mean?" you ask.

"The reports tell us Ching Shee has the ability to replace herself and her crew with exact copies. We've been sleeping for hundreds of years and they've been reproducing themselves. We're being tailed by the latest version of the original crew."

"How close is his ship?" you ask.

"*Her* ship. Ching Shee is a woman and captain of the *Orient Star*," says Captain Wells. "Trig – can you check the ship and get any information you can, including how soon it will be here and anything you can pick up from radio transmissions that might help us understand what we're dealing with."

The Captain turns to you. "We might need to arm ourselves, so find out what we have that can be weaponized. I don't want to wake everyone up for a confrontation. I think we can deal with this robotically. Our ship isn't fast enough to outrun her. We have to be ready."

Trig springs to the console. "I'm on it."

You head off on a transporter to look at the robotic inventory. You remember passing a robot warehouse when you were looking for the animals earlier.

When you enter a small door set inside a larger one there is darkness, but lights start coming on as you move forward. A clanking behind you turns out to be a spider-bot. It's the one you programmed to go out and fix the ship. It's been a bit like your shadow lately.

There are hundreds of different robots standing facing the door. Some are shaped like humans and some like animals. On one side there is a huge snake which would almost fill the corridors of the spaceship. You know it is used for mining.

There is a workshop area in one corner. There is a flit of movement as a little hummingbot flies in buzzing as if it has a problem. The spider-bot moves to the worktable to see what is wrong.

The hummingbot has a wing bent out of shape and the spider-bot gets on to fixing it up. The hummer flies out. At another worktable there's a console where you hope to find an inventory. Again you sense movement behind you. You turn and find several of the robots have stepped forward and moved closer. They must be guarding the robotic system.

"There's another spaceship coming," you say, knowing some robots can understand simple speech. "They might not be friendly. We may need to protect ourselves." You eye the big snake. Perhaps this would be the best machine to bring.

"Ye dinna need such a big brute to fight in close quarters," says a voice from the floor next to you.

It's your spider-bot, and it has a broad Scottish accent. You'd be tempted to laugh if it weren't for the stream of other spider bots appearing from among the bigger robots. Some are large like your spider bot and others are small and delicate like a ladies broach. They are arriving from everywhere, the warehouse, the ceiling, through the door and out of vents – perhaps they've been replicating themselves while everyone slept. They cover the floor and the walls and sit on every surface.

"We'll keep to the shadows and be ready should ye need us."

Wow! A whole Scottish spider army. This will be a great help if the pirates board the *Victoria*. You bow low to the spiders as they scurry off into the ceiling vents and passages.

Knowing you've got help if you need it, you take your transporter back to the bridge and hurriedly explain the spider defense system to the others.

"And it has a Scottish accent?" asks Trig.

He seems more intrigued by this than your security plans. Just as he's about to ask more there's a clanging which heralds the arrival of the *Orient Star* docking below. You hurry down to meet it.

The dock is filled with most of the people you've already met, including the older people from the awake quarters and Dr Ralph. He has Desmond with him and another of the monkeys.

"This is Morris," he says to Trig.

You glance around the dock area – it has very high ceilings and you see some movement here and there – spiders at the ready.

One side of the *Orient Star* is moored to the open iris of the landing dock. The ship is encased in smooth black lacquer with gold colored metalwork. A door slowly opens and a gang plank folds neatly out of the depths of the ship like a tongue. You hear marching feet and then a dozen armored soldiers come down the gang plank bearing long handled axes and wearing light metal armor that covers them head to toe.

It is hard to tell if they are human or robots. They smoothly form a line either side of the door to the *Orient Star*. Next, a carpet rolls down the gangplank – it is a woolen carpet with patterns in dark blues and reds and deep green and gold. Your eye follows it unrolling and then back to the start where the tip of a golden shoe is just stepping onto it.

It is a very small shoe and belongs to a woman who manages to be both small and large all at once. She wears blue silk embroidered garments with deep sleeves, a little like an ornate dressing gown. The silk of her dress is embroidered at the edge with darker blue images of stars and comets and planets. It is as if part of the universe has come to visit you.

She holds her hands together, palms pressed, as she takes small steps down the carpet. Her hands are buried inside the long sleeves. Protruding from her back are the tips of a pair of curved knives. They glint and reflect the landing dock as if the air around her is being sliced up like a broken mirror. Her gown is cinched at the waist by an ornate gold belt. She wears a great deal of white make up and her eyes are colored in pinks and ruby colors. Her dark black hair sits on top of her head in a bun from which jewels glint and shimmer. She treads calmly down the gang plank like she is Queen Victoria herself and quite as though she met up with other space ships every day of the week.

Mesmerized by the person you assume to be Ching Shee you have failed to notice that Captain Wells has made her way to the bottom of the carpet and is bowing in welcome.

One of the visiting guards steps forward and announces: "The honorable explorer: Ching Shee the Ninth," then steps back into formation.

You can't tell from the way he (or she?) spoke, whether the guards are robots or people.

"Our pleasure to meet you. I am Captain Wells." The Captain acts at ease and in charge. Although her uniform is drab in comparison to Ching Shee, it is also smart and practical, and you admire the strong presence Captain Wells has.

Ching Shee eyes the Captain and the surrounds of the dock. You can't help feeling she is taking inventory of the *Victoria* as she begins to speak:

"I too am pleased to meet you," she says to the Captain imperiously, "There must have been some changes among the Britannian people to appoint someone so young and female to the task of commanding this large and most precious vessel."

Captain Wells smiles and offers her arm as if Ching Shee were a trusted friend.

"I am honored to be the first female captain of the *Victoria*. Perhaps you would like to accompany me to somewhere more comfortable where we can exchange news."

Ching Shee gives a regal nod and accepts the Captain's arm.

The Captain is the same height as the pirate as they walk side by side but when your visitor takes steps you see she is wearing high shoes. Ching Shee is about the size of kids you knew at the orphanage. Most of her guards fall in behind her, but two remain at the entrance to the *Orient Star*.

As you and Trig bring up the rear, you can't help wondering what the inside of Ching Shee's ship is like. You grab his arm, slowing him down so the others move ahead, "Trig, can you distract the guards while I send a couple of spider-bots into the *Orient Star*?"

Trig doesn't need asking twice. He instantly understands what a huge advantage it would be to see what's in the visiting ship.

He boldly walks up the gang plank. One of the guards steps up and blocks his way. While Trig talks to the guard, you instruct two spider bots to get inside Ching Shee's vessel. This way if one gets caught, you'll have another in reserve.

While Trig continues his distraction, the first spider-bot lowers itself from a beam above the doorway and slips in over the guards' heads. The second bot walks up *underneath* the gangplank. When the guard standing closest to their ship's entrance steps forward to help his fellow deal with

Trig, it flips up onto the gangplank and joins the other.

"Come on Trig," you say, satisfied your plan has worked, "they don't want visitors. Let's go check out what the captains are up to."

Trig jumps off the gangplank and joins you.

"How'd you go?" he whispers, as you rush down a corridor to catch up with the others.

"Two out of two," you say. "If we need spies we've got them."

The entourage moves to a large room where two chairs have been set up alongside a table with fruit and drinks. Ching Shee's guards stand to attention in a circle around the walls of the room. One guard steps forward and helps her remove the large and shiny knives from her back before she sits down.

"Just ceremonial of course, Captain Wells," she says with a smile.

The two leaders exchange pleasantries for a while. You study the guards, who barely move. Maybe they *are* robots. From time to time you look over to Trig. From something exciting and dangerous, this meeting has become quite boring. Now Captain Wells and the pirate are talking about trade.

"We have a good supply of water on board the *Orient Star*," Ching Shee says as the tea is poured.

"I am not aware that we are in need of water, but I'll ask my engineer to check," replies Captain Wells. "Should we want to trade, what type of goods are you interested in acquiring?"

"We want for very little, but we might identify some trinkets that may be of interest to others," Ching Shee replies. As she speaks she gazes about the room, her glance lands on a hummingbot which has just moved from a perch near the tea trolley to a table at the back.

"Can I ask Captain, how many generations old you are?"

"I'm sorry," says Captain Wells, "I don't understand your question."

Ching Shee looks at her curiously, "I am asking, of course, how many you are removed from your original. I myself relieved the former Ching Shee when she was 54 years old. I am Ching Shee the ninth. What about you?"

The captain is evasive in her answer – she has no reason to trust Ching Shee. It appears that although she has a faster ship she does not have the sleep technology you have.

"We've been traveling a long time – I'm not as aware of our history as you are." The ninth Ching Shee doesn't notice that the captain has avoided her question, she is looking at the corner of the room.

"What is that?" she asks, pointing.

Captain Wells follows Ching Shee's eyes and sees Desmond's game. "Oh that's just a game."

Ching Shee signals and one of her guards moves the table closer. "I don't know it. Demonstrate please."

Ching Shee's request makes you uneasy. It sounds a lot

like an order.

The captain looks at you and shrugs, "Can you play?"

"Perhaps Her Eminence will be amused if we invite Desmond to play?" you suggest. He's actually the only other player you know. You sit at the game table and instruct a hummingbot to find Desmond. It doesn't have to go far – it turns out Desmond is in the very next room, presumably wanting to get the game back. When he strolls in, one of Ching Shee's guards takes a step back and gasps. So, you think, they aren't robots.

Desmond walks up to you and sits down at the game. You both begin to select your pieces. First your main piece – you select a dolphin. Because you've picked a water creature Desmond changes the boardscape so that a large portion is sea. He picks a killer whale. He gets to pick the partner – he thinks for a while and selects a white heron. A bird is a good idea, you start looking at birds as well.

"You need a bird too," says Ching Shee, agreeing with your strategy. She brings her chair closer and looks at the pieces. Her guards crowd around too. One takes off their helmet. You look at Ching Shee and you look at the guard – they could almost be twin sisters. Ching Shee sees you looking.

"She's one of the *nearly* Ching Shees – she is 'the same recipe'. She gets to be an honor guard and also to play games with me."

"How do you stop from getting mixed up?" The question

comes from Trig, it seems like the ice is broken and everyone has stopped being so formal.

"She does not have this," says Ching Shee, rolling up her sleeve. Her arm is tattooed with a blue dragon. The head covers her wrist and the body coils up toward her elbow and beyond. "Only one of us wears the dragon. The seventh Ching Shee only wore the dragon for three days."

"What happened to her?" you ask.

"The eighth Ching Shee happened to her," purrs Ching Shee the ninth.

Desmond grunts, reminding you to pick your companion piece. You select an eagle and then the game begins. You start out by exploring territory and scoping out allies and enemies. A forest fire drives a bunch of animals your way and makes their living space smaller, there's a conflict and the monkeys start to take over all the spaces the birds nested in. If you can get some more territory you can sort out space for everyone and maybe if you could grow more trees… The game continues and is just as engrossing as the first time you played it.

"We have not seen a planet like this one in your game," says one of the guards, as you all munch on sandwiches an hour later.

"Like what?" Trig asks.

"A planet so full of life. Usually it's just water or just rocks."

"You've explored new planets?" The captain asks, leaning

towards the guard.

Ching Shee shoots a glance at the guard then shrugs. "We've mapped a lot of new territory," Ching Shee says. "We get around, and we trade for information too. Perhaps we've found something you'd like to trade for: Information."

"And what would you like in return?" purrs the captain.

"I like this monkey and this game," Ching Shee states like a spoilt child. "That's what I want."

Desmond looks at Ching Shee. Does he understand? You think he does. Would the captain trade them for knowledge? Desmond taps you on the shoulder to remind you that you're in the middle of a game and it's your turn.

Desmond has joined up with a pod of killer whales and a flock of herons – he's playing to win and has your dolphins separated from the eagles. As you try to find another ally Desmond makes his final move. You are completely surrounded. The chimp has won. Behind you, Ching Shee's guards clap.

"My turn!" Ching Shee cries.

As she takes your place you leave the room with Trig. You want to see what the spiders in Ching Shee's ship have been up to. You duck into a service room and tap into the robotics system. With a bit of fiddling you manage to get a transmission from your spider-bots. One is on a wall looking down on row after row of what look like sleeping pods. Inside each pod is a girl at various stages of growth – this must be the cloning system. You tell the spider-bot to move on.

Next you find the feed from the other spider-bot. It is in a large library, filled with lacquered shelving, and on the walls are star charts. The bot is making copies of them all. The charts are covered in Chinese writing – you can't understand much of it but someone on board will have the skills to read the maps. A shiver of excitement runs through you. This information could help you figure out where the *Victoria* should head to find a planet to settle – or at least areas which are yet unexplored. You also feel a bit awful for stealing information.

Meanwhile, the second spider-bot has found its way deeper into the *Orient Star*. You see a long corridor with two guards at one end. A series of doors with barred windows make this look like some kind of jail. The guards are facing each other across a small table and are deeply engrossed in a game.

You instruct the spider to look inside the first door. It climbs stealthily across the ceiling and then lowers itself down to the bars. Because of the angle you are viewing everything from upside down.

Inside sits a man reading a book. He has brown skin. The man looks at the door and sees the spider-bot. He waves and gestures for the spider to come forward. You let the spider know it can approach.

"Who are you?" asks the man, he has a swirling tattoo on

his face. "You don't look like *Orient Star* technology. Are you a spy?" He bustles around and writes a note. He holds it up to the spider-bot.

I am held captive by the pirate Ching Shee.

"Well little spider bot – perhaps if you're reporting back to someone you can tell them about me?"

The man in the cell doesn't realize you can hear what he's saying. You instruct your spider bot to open the door, but as it is about to do so, a commotion outside makes it pause.

You look through the bars cautiously through the spider-bot's eyes. It's Desmond. He's being marched down the corridor with both the game and his friend Morris. Ching Shee has kidnapped them!

You instruct the spider to stay put and check up on the one that is copying the maps. It's finishing up and sending the information back to the *Victoria*. You have nearly all the transmission when it cuts off. You jump on a transporter and head toward the bridge hoping to find Captain Wells so you can tell her about Desmond. As you turn a corner you find her striding towards you.

"Engineer, do you have spider-bots on the *Orient Star?*" asks Captain Wells.

You're about to tell her what you've seen when Dr Ralph arrives on a transporter.

"Desmond and Morris have disappeared," Dr Ralph cries. "Morris is really shy – she hardly goes anywhere. I think the pirates might have her."

"They do," you say. Then you tell the two of them about the prisoner you found.

"I suspect they're planning to clone Desmond and Morris," says Dr Ralph, "but it won't work. Those chimps have years of learning using the sleep jelly. Clones will just be normal monkeys."

Trig arrives. "That woman and her clone army have just taken off!"

"The bridge. Quickly!" says the captain. "Fill us in while we move."

"It's hopeless," Trig says, "she's a much faster ship and she knows where she's going."

"Desmond and Morris are just babies!" Dr Ralph moans. "They'll be confused and scared. I don't know what they'll do."

Once on the bridge, you check that the *Orient Star's* maps have been copied to the *Victoria's* library.

You grab Trig's sleeve. "Hey take a look at this data we got from Ching Shee's ship. If we overlay it on what we mapped earlier can you decode the rest?"

Trig boots up another console and scours the maps.

"This is brilliant. Thankfully, quite a lot of it isn't Chinese, just standard nautical mapping signals. The pirates must have adapted a mixture of old seafaring mapping notation and newer mapping."

"Really?" you say. "Does that work?"

"It sort of does – ancient seafaring used the stars you

know. Modern space mapping just adds a 3rd dimension. Basically, these Chinese mappers were just expanding the known universe like they were a sailing ship in the sky."

"Never mind that," Dr Ralph cuts in. "Do you have any idea where they're going? Desmond and Morris are like my own children, we need to get them back."

"What's this supposed to be?" you ask.

Drawn amidst the technical notes and figures is a picture of a dragon's head and a long tail.

"It's a comet," Trig says, "See, the observation dates are written along the tail. They'd use those to figure out when the comet was due again. Then they could make sure they were out of its path."

You stare at the tiny mathematical notations as Trig continues to compare your own ship's maps and the new ones. You idly make calculations to figure the frequency of the comet's path.

Trig stabs his finger on Ching Shee's maps. "OK. We're here and Ching Shee took off that way. There's a planet in this sector here that's been well mapped. It's not very far away. I think this mark represents a space station of some sort. She might be heading there."

As Trig expands on his theory, an idea forms in your mind. It has to do with the comet you found marked on Ching Shee's map.

Your thoughts are interrupted by the Captain. "Dr Ralph, I'm dreadfully sorry but even though we know the direction

Ching Shee's gone, we'll never be able to catch her ship."

"What if we could?" you ask.

All eyes turn to you.

You touch Ching Shee's map, tracing your finger along the dragon's tail. "This comet is due in about two days and it's going in the right direction. What if we hitched a ride? If my calculations are correct, we'll get there before her and have time to check out the space station and perhaps the planet. There's something else too."

You pause for effect, feeling quite proud of your clever plan, and wanting everyone to realize how brilliant you are.

"Well, spit it out Engineer!" says Captain Wells.

"If we get close to her ship, I could get the spiders to create a bit of mayhem."

The sense of despair on the bridge is gone. Everyone gets to work immediately. You set off to make a huge harpoon. Your plan is to hook the comet, get dragged along at high speed, and then cut yourself loose and slingshot the *Victoria* ahead of the *Orient Star*.

Three hours later you have a full complement of robots working on the harpoon and Trig has made several sets of calculations for the initial strike and the release. When you're dragged into the comet's tail you might lose control of the ship so you've designed a manual system that will allow you to release the *Victoria* when the time is right.

At the heart of the harpoon is an exploding pin with a cooling system to keep it in place.

"What's that for?" Dr Ralph asks as he puts a cup of hot chocolate and a plate of biscuits on the desk beside you.

"Most comets are big chunks of ice. If that's the case, we'll hook it and then fuse the harpoon onto it," you tell him.

"Thanks for trying to get Desmond and Morris back," says Dr Ralph.

"Are you kidding? Desmond has beaten me twice at that game – I want to get my own back." You laugh. "Besides, we can't have Ching Shee out there taking whatever she wants. If we keep traveling on, who's to say she wouldn't be back for something else. If she ever found out about the sleep jelly she'd want that too. Who knows what havoc she'd make then."

Dr Ralph nods gravely. "If we catch her, what do you think we should do with her?"

"That's for the Captain to decide," you say. You haven't really had time to think about that part of the operation. As the two of you eat, you stare into space. Somewhere out there, in the calm blue tranquility, a moon–sized comet is hurtling towards you at tremendous speed. Snaring the comet has absorbed your mind for hours. You suddenly realize how tired you are and yawn.

"I'll keep watch," Dr Ralph says. "Go get some sleep."

Seven hours later a spider-bot comes to wake you. You go to check that everything is ready for launch.

A big net is positioned across the comet's path. When the

comet hits, the net will wrap around it and set off the harpoon.

You check your console. "Everything is ready, Captain."

"Let's do this," Captain Wells says.

A team of twelve hummers escort the net outside and stretch it out. When they get back inside you don't have long to wait.

"Comet ahoy!" shouts Trig, as his sensors pick up something approaching.

You look out a porthole but can only see a small bright dot.

A robot comes onto the bridge along with Dr Ralph. Everyone tucks into a meal as the bright light goes from a pin prick to the size of a tennis ball. It almost doubles in size by the time you finish your meal. The next job is to batten down the ship. It will be a bumpy ride when you catch the comet.

You close down the irises, leaving only the super reinforced window of the bridge open. It has a dark screen installed to act like a giant pair of sunglasses. You've just strapped yourself into flight chairs when you hear the comet coming. It reminds you of a glass chandelier outside being tinkled in the wind. The noise increases to the sort of rattling and clanging you'd hear in a storm. The comet hits the net. Presumably the harpoon digs in because there is a lurching tug and you are suddenly streaming through space in the comet's ice storm of a tail. You've done it! You are racing faster than anyone has ever gone before.

"Start the count," you tell Trig, but you can see he's already on it.

You've got to withstand the tow for four minutes and then cut loose. Time has never gone as slowly. There's a tooth rattling vibration through your chair. It will be the same everywhere on the *Victoria*.

"I hope this crazy idea doesn't get us all killed," you say.

"Three minutes left," yells Trig.

"Really? We're not even a third of the way?" Your fingernails are cutting into the leather upholstery of the chair.

Then Trig calls out, "One minute."

OK nearly there. The ship has held up so far. There are no lights going red on the consoles. In fact the electrics are all still alive, you aren't flying blind at all.

"Thirty seconds, twenty nine, twenty eight…" Trig counts down.

It's nearly time to release from the comet.

"Release," you say calmly enough when the count hits zero but inside you are a mess of emotions. At first nothing happens but then the noise abates and the vibrating slows and eventually stops altogether – you are free from the comet.

"Full power!" the Captain says. "Engage all thrusters."

The ship's engines are almost silent compared to the racket of being towed by the comet. The quiet is like velvet to your ears. All over the ship, robots will be checking for damage, including your army of spiders. You unbuckle from your chair and raise the main window. Outside is a new section of the universe.

Trig has added Ching Shee's maps to the *Victoria's* own, and he's checking where you are.

"We've come further than we thought. I reckon we have a few days lead on the pirates," Trig says. "That space station is close by and beyond that is the new planet."

"How long to the station?" asks the Captain.

Trig checks his calculations. "Two hours, twelve minutes and sixteen seconds."

The Captain nods. "We don't know if they're friends or foe, Trig. If we can communicate with them from here let's do it. I'd like to keep a respectful distance until we know more."

All the exhilaration you felt at jaunting across the universe fades. You've still got to prepare to face the pirates.

"We've got a radio signal coming from the space station," Trig says.

While preparing for the comet ride, a number of new people were woken up. Some were ready to help with any damage to the ship and others were to be part of exploration and communication parties. One of the communicators comes onto the bridge now. Like you and Trig she wears the ship's uniform and she's managed to make it look quite smart. You look down at yourself, you're distinctly rumpled after a few days action.

She salutes Trig, assuming he must be the captain. He shakes his head a little and points at Captain Wells. The newcomer blushes and curtsies to the Captain.

"Pardon me ma'am, language specialist reporting for duty. I'm Flora ma'am."

"Good timing," says Captain Wells. The Captain introduces herself and the rest of you to the newcomer. "We've just had a transmission from that object over there."

Everyone goes silent as Trig tunes in to the message. The language is one you don't know. The others, apart from Flora, seem just as confused as you are by the strange sounding message.

Flora's face is one of concentration as she listens "They're saying the planet below has terrible monsters ma'am. They want to know if we're planning on settling there. They've had a bit of bad luck it seems."

"What language are they speaking Flora?"

"It's Maori ma'am. From New Zealand."

The Captain frowns. "Isn't it because of those upstarts that we're colonizing way out here?"

You must have learned some history while sleeping. "That's right Captain. The Maori took their revolution from New Zealand to Australia and then on to the Americas. They own half of planet Earth."

"And now they're out here too," the Captain says. "Ask them why, if the planet is no good, they haven't moved on.

Oh and check if they've come across Ching Shee."

Flora steps up to the microphone and begins talking. You are amused to see she flutters her hands about as she does so – although the recipients won't see any of the actions she's making. There's a pause as the people on the other side digest what she's said. When the reply comes there is a brief song and then a woman's voice continues. This time the speech is in English:

"Greetings people of the *Victoria* from Britannia. We are of the tribe Ngati Kahungunu from Aotearoa and we have travelled to these stars that herald Matariki - the beginning of new growth each year.

"Your speaker tells us that you met the warrior Ching Shee and she has taken something of yours. We are sorry about that. Ching Shee has taken something of ours too – our chief. She has also dismantled our craft."

The travelers explain they were setting up a mission to populate the planet below when Ching Shee stole their chief and sabotaged their space station.

"Now Ching Shee says she will only help us colonize the planet if we agree to her terms. We are to be her slaves. We do not even know if our chief is still alive."

"Tell them he's alive!" you interrupt. "They must be talking about the man I saw in the cell." You bring up a recording of what the spider-bot recorded and send the clip over to the space station.

There are exclamations from the other vessel. Things

become a lot friendlier. You arrange to dock and work on a plan together. You must hurry. The Maori explorers are expecting Ching Shee to return soon.

On board the space station you find an efficient little set up with hydroponic gardens in every room. The floors are clear and you can see fish swimming under your feet. It is like being in a huge glass bottomed boat. The walls are covered in moss and there are plants everywhere. Unlike the opulence of the *Victoria*, this ship, with its forests and fern and gardens everywhere, is practical and beautiful in a very natural way.

"We traded for water with Ching Shee several times – but then she double crossed us," explains Aroha, the woman you had been speaking with by radio. "She has taken parts of our engine to prevent us from taking the space station down to the planet. Without it, and all the equipment aboard, we won't survive against the creatures down there."

After some discussion, there is a decision to use the element of surprise as Ching Shee doesn't know you are here.

The *Victoria* offloads a lot of spider-bots onto the Maori space station. A number of them cling to the hull outside as well.

If your plan works there will be no harm to any people and, hopefully, no harm to your robots. There is still time to wait, everyone is eager to learn about the planet you are orbiting.

Aroha shows you the maps they have made of the planet's surface. There are many volcanic islands. On the continents there are huge animals. Some are herbivores and eat the massive trees that form a canopy across this world, but there are predators too.

"And I wouldn't want to meet one of them down a dark alley," says Trig.

"Tell me about it," you say. "But I reckon some of the robots we have on the *Victoria*, would be a match for these monsters."

Maybe settlers from the *Victoria* could carve out some territory where they could be safe and learn to get along with these huge land animals.

As you consider the possibilities, you get to work fixing the space station. Once again you thank your lucky stars that you have been given the training to be an engineer while you slept. The *Victoria* might be old technology but you've essentially cracked time travel and the problem of passing on knowledge, something neither Ching Shee nor the Maori explorers have done. Your new companions were all born in space.

The Maori space station is high tech but you are able to figure it out. With parts from the *Victoria* the *Takitimu* is soon mobile again.

"But we won't move the ship yet. We want it to be a surprise," smiles Kupe, their navigator. "I'm looking forward to getting the upper hand with Ching Shee."

You find yourself alone with Captain Wells and broach the subject of trying to settle the planet below. "It might have big monsters but it also has water and plant life. I wonder, if we pooled our resources with these settlers, could we make a go of it?"

Captain Wells nods, "That's certainly worth considering. We can't stay between the stars forever. Even if we put down some of our passengers we'll be spreading our risk."

At the end of the day the crew working on the space station re-join the *Victoria* and the ship takes off to the other side of the planet leaving you and your spider bot army to wait for the *Orient Star*. You fill in the time checking the position and programming the spiders, too excited to sleep.

"Will ye get some rest?" says your favorite spider. "We cannae have yee fallin' asleep in what is to come." It jumps on your bunk and scuttles up to your pillow, tapping it with two legs. You get in the bunk and your robot starts a story:

"Once upon a time there was a veeery intelligent robot shaped like a spider, and it had a lot of wee friends…"

Your eyes grow heavy and you start to nod off even though you are trying to follow the robot's tale. How on Earth did it get programmed to tell bedtime stories?

Aroha and Kupe wake you up with hot food and drink. You have noticed they mostly eat vegetables and fish. For breakfast you have hot potato cakes with salmon. "Delicious."

After a quick shower you put on the uniform of the

Maori passengers to be as unobtrusive as possible. Then you wait as Ching Shee's ship nears. When it is within hailing distance Aroha opens up a frequency and speaks out to the pirate.

"Greetings *Orient Star*."

"Hello most unfortunate stranded travelers," chimes Ching Shee's voice. "Are you ready to be rescued by my most generous self and live your lives in gratitude of my benevolence?"

Aroha keeps her voice steady and calm as she replies to the pirate. This part is critical to your plan.

"We have given your offer much thought as we've floated around this planet and have decided defeat is almost inevitable. However, we know Your Eminence enjoys games. Therefore, we challenge you to a game of your choice – chess, backgammon, cards – you choose. The victor will rule the planet and the loser will obey them in all things. What do you say?"

There is silence for a few seconds. Clearly the pirate had not expected such an offer but you know her ego will tempt her to take up the challenge.

Sure enough, her voice comes back to you, this time with a note of cunning in it. "I am a benevolent ruler and a wise one. We will begin the glorious history of our settlement of this planet with a game as you suggest. Let it always be said that I, Ching Shee the ninth, was reasonable and clever in all things. Prepare for boarding. I will challenge you in one

Earth hour."

The pirate has given you time you don't want to waste. Quickly you contact your spiders aboard the *Orient Star*. They begin broadcasting the ship's schematics to the *Victoria* and you send over their final instructions. When all the information required for your plan has been transmitted, you ask the two spy spider-bots to locate Desmond, Morris and the Maori chief.

The Chief's voice comes through a few minutes later. "Aroha? Is that you? Kupe?"

You explain how you have joined forces with his people to rescue him and let him know what to expect.

When Desmond appears on your monitor he doesn't seem too distressed and is just finishing a game with one of Ching Shee's body guards. Morris is playing nearby. She glances at the spider-bot on the ceiling then gets up and walks over to the window and gestures to the space station outside.

Desmond doesn't appear to have noticed the bot.

The spider bot moves closer to the table where Desmond and the guard are playing. You can hear what the guard is saying.

"With her new slaves, Ching Shee is going to set up a mining operation on the planet. First she'll kill the large animals and then she'll gather the riches under its surface."

The guard speaks of this with such certainty that you know Ching Shee must have done this before. What a terrible thing to do – a good planet is hard to find and she would plunder it and ruin it!

More guards come into the room just as Desmond claims victory. One of them has a big plate of fruit. They take away Desmond's game, but he's distracted by the food and another guard setting up a game of chess. At least Desmond doesn't look desperately unhappy.

Things are happening exactly as you expected.

You lose picture quality as the spider moves into a small duct. The bot has work to do.

Meanwhile on the space station, a gang plank is lowered for Ching Shee and her guards. From your perch at the scanners you see the pirate captain make a similar entrance to the one she made on the *Victoria*.

Aroha and Kupe meet her at the end of the carpet. They start an interesting welcoming ceremony which you wish you could watch more closely, but you are busy deploying the spiders. The two spiders on the Chinese ship will open an airlock to let them in.

"Ah! There they are now," you say to yourself as you watch the progress on the monitor.

The spiders move carefully – metal on metal can make quite a clang and you want to surprise the pirates.

Aroha and Kupe talk with Ching Shee. She grandly gestures at Desmond's game which is being carried from the *Orient Star*.

Aroha and Kupe look dismayed, as if they had not

expected this game. But in fact, you have told them all about it and coached them as much as you could on how it is played. They need to play the game long enough for the spiders to do their job if your plan is to work.

Kupe and Aroha offer a meal to Ching Shee but she declines – it would have been nice if she'd had time to socialize before enslaving these people but you hope you'll have enough time to do what you need to while the game is going on.

Time is at a premium. Already Ching Shee's guards are setting up the board and arranging the pieces.

The last of the spiders are now aboard the *Orient Star* and the airlocks are shut. As the bots make their way into the depths of the ship you monitor their progress.

In the ceiling of the bridge a massive rewiring operation is going on. The spiders are establishing their own control center. The pirate controls will be useless. Meanwhile several spiders have entered the cloning facility. They lock the doors and sit on top of the tanks. Two can play the hostage game.

Speaking of games, the game aboard the Maori vessel is well underway. Kupe is playing Ching Shee and he looks anxious. Never mind that he is supposedly playing for the freedom of his people, the game is complex and Ching Shee is winning. She has the benefit of having played every day against Desmond. The two opponents play with grim determination.

You tell the spiders to open the Chief's cell and watch

through one of your spider eyes as he gingerly steps out into a corridor. There are no guards – everyone is either over on the Maori vessel or up in the games room watching the contest from a live feed.

Desmond and Morris are in the games room. Desmond is interested but Morris is looking round. She knows something is going on. She notices when a door opens and a spider waves a leg for her to follow.

Morris takes Desmond's hand and the two saunter out. In the deserted corridor Morris points to a spider-bot and Desmond understands something is happening.

The spiders take them to meet the other captive. The chief looks completely confused when he meets up with Desmond and Morris.

Morris points to the spider and then at a passing pirate. She puts her finger to her lips.

That seems to be enough for him to know she is on his side. They head towards the open airlock between the *Orient Star* and the Maori vessel but the entry is blocked by guards who point them back the way they came. They sit a little way off and wait patiently.

"I've won!" Ching Shee says with a smile. "Now your children will say how Ching Shee the ninth won their loyalty. Now we will raze the planet below of its large and useless inhabitants and set up a profitable mining business to expand our empire into the next galaxy."

This is your moment, you step out from the control room

where you have been concealed.

"I'm sorry, but you won't be taking these people as your loyal servants today."

Ching Shee squints at you. "Don't I know you?"

"Engineer of the *Victoria* ma'am, at these people's service. I'm sorry to inform you that your ship is suffering an infestation of spiders. They've rewired your ship and they have your cloning room under their control. I'm willing to help you get rid of them but first I need you to release all your hostages."

Just then a guard from Ching Shee's ship stumbles into the room and makes a signal. Ching Shee stands and starts barking orders.

One of the guards draws a sword. Faster than the guard can step toward you, a spider drops from the ceiling and administers a swift jab to the guard's neck. The guard crumples to the floor.

Another guard puts her hand on her sword and the same thing happens. Ching Shee and her entourage look up warily. The ceiling is alive with spiders!

"Back to the ship!" she cries.

"I'm sorry ma'am I'm going to have to ask you to listen to me," you say, walking forward and standing next to Aroha and Kupe. "The spiders in your ship have disabled your bridge, you have no power and you can't go anywhere. That's not all, you'll find a spider sitting above every cloning tank on the ship. If you don't start listening there may be no

Ching Shee the tenth."

At this the pirate captain starts to fume and spit orders.

"Kill that engineer now!" she shrieks, stamping her foot. None of the guards move to follow her command, they all saw what happened to their fellows.

Ching Shee turns to you. "What do you want?" she hisses, cold as ice.

"For starters I'd like the safe return of the chief and my friends Desmond and Morris. Order your guards to return to your ship and send them over. Then we'll talk."

"I'm not handing them over. I won dominion over these people fairly. I won this game!" she points at the board. "You are bound by your British honor to give me these people and their ship. I will give you your monkeys in return."

"I think you're confusing me with someone who didn't grow up in an orphanage. Someone who wasn't caught stealing bread and sent to prison. There's no honor when you are hungry, Ching Shee. Hand over your prisoners. I'm not asking again."

"Ahh, so you are a pirate at heart," the pirate tries one last time. "You have humble beginnings like the first Ching Shee. You should join me. Together we could own the universe and take the Earth. We can replicate ourselves over and over until it is done. What do you say?"

"I asked nicely," you say, tiring of her antics, "put her to sleep, thank you."

Ching Shee screams like a banshee and dives toward a sword but the spiders are fast. Two jump on her and strike. She crumples to the floor. She looks like a child who fell asleep after a tantrum.

There is a clatter of swords as one by one each of the guards drops their weapon. Helmets are taken off and the Maori crew gasp as they see that face after face is the same – all copies of Ching Shee. One of the Chinese crew steps cautiously forward.

"Noble warrior, ah engineer. We have heard what you said. It is time for a new leader and new ways – would you consider leading our crew?"

As you are digesting this request you see the *Victoria* arrive from where she has been hidden behind the planet. There is a burst of static and then you hear the vessel being hailed.

The crew scrambles to pick up Ching Shee and take her to a cell. Then they take the swords and weapons from her surrendering crew and lock them in a storage unit.

When Desmond and Morris arrive there's chaos as the two of them recognize you and rush over. When Dr Ralph arrives he weeps openly when he sees Desmond and Morris again.

Everyone moves on to the bigger *Victoria* for a feast and to swap stories. Captain Wells hints at some interesting developments. Has she more information about the planet below?

There is laughter and chatter all over the *Victoria*. It takes you a while before you find Trig zooming about the lower corridors on a transporter.

"Well done!" he yells as he hurtles toward you and leaps off. "Did the Captain tell you we've scouted the planet? We've found large islands without big animals. Did she tell you we might be settling here?"

"No," you say, "She said we'd swap stories over a feast. I've been looking for you. Let's go eat."

"Right," says Trig. "Try and look surprised when she tells you alright?"

Sounds like you have some decisions ahead of you. Do you take off as the leader of the pirate ship or settle down on the new planet? You've made some great friends and had adventures that will be told for generations to come.

You jump on the transporter behind Trig and practice your surprised face as you head to the landing bay where the feast will be served. It's the only place big enough for so many people.

You slide open the door a crack hoping to make a quiet entrance but one of Ching Shee's ex-guards sees you and springs up to salute. Soon all the guards rise and bow and you're waved up to the main table. Trig settles into a spot right next to you and the captain.

The Captain starts telling you, Aroha and Kupe about the land the *Victoria* has found. "Why don't you look surprised Engineer?"

This part of the story is over but there are many other paths you can take. Do you:

Go back to the beginning and try another path? **P1**

Or

Go to the list of choices and pick another place to start? **P172**

Go back to sleep again

You have chosen to sleep again, sleep is so wonderful. Who would want to be awake when you can stay in blissful sleep? In your dreams your sleep chamber is moved to a new location and you dream of having the option to work on a new planet or to stay sleeping. Sleep is so good. So comfortable.

In your dreams you are working in a mine. You are always tired. It seems odd that you keep dreaming of mining. Shouldn't you be learning new things while you sleep? Next to you is another miner. He's very old. It's odd you are dreaming of older people when sleeping chambers preserve you in sleep.

Next to you the old miner staggers and sways with fatigue. "Rest," you say, but he doesn't hear you.

You put out your hand to steady him as he sways again and look around. You are deep in a mineshaft surrounded by other miners. They are all old like the miner next to you. There are old men and old women chipping away at a large seam of coal.

The old man sits down, he's had it. A robot comes down a railway line with a cart. It gently lifts the miner into the cart and starts to take him away.

"Where are you taking him?" you ask.

The robot pauses and turns to scan you. Did you do the right thing asking the robot about the old man?

"Are you awake?" the robot asks.

You think about the question. Surely this is a dream, but then maybe it isn't. It seems very odd that someone in a dream would ask you if you were awake. How do you answer a question you're not sure of?

You have a couple of choices. Do you:

Tell the robot you are awake? **P118**

Or

Tell the robot you are asleep? **P117**

You tell the robot you are asleep

"That's right sleeper, you're dreaming. You never wanted to wake and do any work and you never will have to wake. I am authorized to send you back into a deep sleep. If at any time you want to wake up, you have only to tell me. We treat everyone with kindness on the new planet, sleepers and non-sleepers alike. Go back to sleep now."

You are feeling very drowsy and your mind struggles to think about what you've just heard. You remember there were times when you have been asked if you want to wake and you chose sleep. Why wake when you can travel between the stars and never age? Sleepily you wonder what will happen at the end of the journey. What will the settlers do with people who don't want to wake...

That's the end of this part of the story. What would you like to do now?

Go back to the beginning? **P1**

Or

Go to the list of choices and start reading from another part of the story? **P172**

You decide to tell the robot you are awake

"Yes, I'm awake," you say, stepping forward and staring into the robot's scanner. It pauses and relays information back to the central computer.

"Sleeper, do you want to be awake?" asks the robot.

You think about all the time you might have spent sleeping, the times you have had opportunities to wake and didn't. It's time to get on with your life.

"Yes," you say. "I want to be awake."

The robot sprays you in the face with a sharp smelling vapor. Your knees buckle and you fall backwards into another cart. You follow behind the old miner being carted up the railway tracks to the surface. On the way up you see old miners sitting in carts as they are wheeled down. They have a vacant expression on their faces. They don't seem unhappy, it's more like they're dreaming.

The walls begin to appear as natural light filters down from above. Tracks lead up towards a round circle of light. The increased light hurts your eyes.

You come out squinting to an alien landscape. The sky is a funny sort of purple and large red bats glide across the sky. As the smells of coal and grease and steam from the tunnel fade, you start to smell other things. The air is very different to the air on Earth and to the sterile air of the space ship.

Your little cart is still being pushed along by the robot. You enter a building and a man in a suit with a top hat greets you. He has a handle bar moustache and, at about 40, is the youngest person you've seen today.

"You must be the sleeper who has decided to wake up!" he cries and shakes your hand. "Welcome to Victorious. Welcome to our utopia. I am one of the great grandchildren of the original settlers. They broke in the land here and started the coal mines."

He babbles on, enthusiastically talking of the settlement of the planet, but you aren't listening. You have caught sight of your reflection in the window. You see an old face and gray hair. Slowly you look down to your wrinkled and liver-spotted hands. Old hands. He is still talking:

"…and then many of the sleepers said they didn't want to wake up. It seemed you got used to sleeping and preferred it. At first we let people sleep on in the cryo-chambers but then my grandfather had the bright idea to get some labor in exchange for the sleep. Unfortunately when you're sleep-working your body ages. But you'll be pleased to know that while you've been mining here you've cleared your debt, worked off your sentence AND made some savings. We've saved your money prudently. You now have enough set aside to retire!"

You look out the window. There's a new world beyond the mine. Huge birds circle mountains carpeted in strange plants. There will be rivers nobody has ever traveled, and new animals, and so much more to explore. You don't have much time left but you want to see as much of it as you can.

You've reached the end of this branch of the story but that's not a problem – there's plenty more story left: Do you want to:

Go Back to the beginning and try another path? **P1**

Or

Go to the list of choices and choose another place to start reading? **P172**

Wait for another mission or to land on the new planet

You don't know if months or many years have passed before you hear another voice asking you to wake.

"Sleeper. Do you want to wake up?"

You don't have to wake. You can keep sleeping. You are such a good sleeper. You vaguely remember something about a space ship. About traveling somewhere. That's it, you are on the space ship *Victoria*. You're traveling a long way away on an adventure. One day you'll get to a new planet. Maybe you're already there?

"Sleeper. Do you want to wake up?"

That's right. You can choose to wake up on the way. You can have adventures. But if you stay awake too long you'll be old when you get to the new plant or never get there at all. You won't get to spend your life exploring it.

You need to choose. Do you:

Wake up? **P122**

Or

Stay asleep? **P115**

Wake up for an adventure

You are swimming in a large tank. Something is following you like a shadow but you aren't worried. You sense that your tank mate is a large fish-like creature, just like you.

You know you used to be human, but being like this feels ... wonderful. You just wish you had more water to swim in.

You beat your fluke and send your sleek body surging up to the surface. As you leap above the water you expel air from your blowhole and take in a fresh supply. Several humans are sitting on a platform at the top of your tank.

"Sleeper, I'm Dr Alan. Can you understand me?"

The speaker is a young man in a white coat. He's very tall. You click once for yes. It's something you learned in your sleep. Sitting next to Dr Alan is someone you know very well.

It is you. Human-you.

Human–you is standing next to a girl with tight black curls and a mischievous grin and they both look pretty excited.

You remember waking up and being asked about undertaking a mission. You agreed to have your mind copied into the body of a dolphin so you can explore a new planet. It's strange to see your old self there. The girl next to you must have shared her mind with a dolphin too.

Dolphin-you shoots a stream of water at human-you. Human-you and the curly haired girl try and duck away but end up wet and laughing.

Dolphin-you lets out a laugh that sounds like a high pitched spluttering whistle.

The man in the white coat frowns. "Yes, very funny. But we're not here to lark about. This is quite serious."

You and the other dolphin stop and listen.

"Your human bodies are still safe here on the spaceship as you can see. We have shared your minds with a dolphin. The dolphin mind is asleep and we are just drawing from its instincts. All its memories and thinking processes have been completely suppressed."

As you listen to the scientist explain why you are now in the body of a dolphin, you look at your old self on the platform, yet feel perfectly normal as a dolphin.

Your human self leaves with the girl. Then Dr Alan explains how the human-you and the girl will wait on the ship to find out how the mission goes.

The Doctor throws you a fish which you snap up greedily. "I'm calling the planet Atlantica – partly because of the lost city of Atlantis and partly because of our beloved Britannia."

Another person climbs onto the platform and joins Dr Alan. You recognize him too, but it isn't a pleasant memory. It's the scar-faced youth you met when you were trying out for space transportation that first time. He very nearly ruined your chances for no reason at all.

You try to say something about it, but all you can do is make whistles and clicks.

"Sleeper, are you asking about the Inventor?" asks the white coated Dr Alan. He gestures towards scar-face. Surely, you think, he isn't the Inventor? The Inventor is an old man who designed the space ship you are traveling in and many of the wonders on board. His own father invented sleep jelly.

Dr Alan explains. "This is the body of the criminal Moriarty but I can assure you Moriarty's mind does not rule this body any more. Moriarty paid that price for his crimes. His body now carries the mind of the great man who made our journey possible. The Inventor was too old to sleep in space so his mind was transferred into this body. Do you understand?"

You click to say yes.

As Dr Alan tells you more about your mission you keep looking at the face of Moriarty – it is difficult to trust that face despite what you've heard.

"The ship has come very close to a new planet," Dr Alan says. "It is mostly covered in water. We've decided a dolphin is the best scout for this largely aquatic environment. There are other planets in this solar system, but for the mission to be successful we need to pick the best one to settle on. You are going to be the first explorers."

"Lucky us," whistles your tank companion in the language of dolphins.

Her clicking is very pleasing to your ears. You've never noticed how gruff and unmelodic humans sound when they talk.

"Hello?" you whistle back.

"Hello Proudfin," says the dolphin next to you.

"Proudfin?"

"That's what I'm calling you. Any objection?"

"That's fine … Longtail," you say.

From the quick series of clicks she makes, you know she likes the name you just gave her. It has two meanings. Not only does the other dolphin have a long tail but the tales of your adventures will be carried a long way.

"Listen up you two," Dr Alan continues. "A small space ship, an 'explorer', is to be sent to the planet below. The explorer will also carry robots. They will build a radio station for you to broadcast back to the *Victoria*. You and Longtail will be placed in special tubes of sleep jelly. The jelly will help cushion you in space and also provide oxygen in the same way it does when you sleep. Once you land on the new planet you'll explore and report back via a radio station.

The Inventor steps closer to the edge of your tank. "We appreciate what you are doing. Your exploration will help us decide if we can settle down there on Atlantica. You are sentinels for all of us. Travel safely."

His voice lacks the sneering tone of the prisoner you met on Earth. Maybe you should just relax about him. Besides, you're heading off on a major journey.

In quick order, you are transferred to special capsules filled with sleep jelly. Then your capsules are sealed and placed in the explorer. It isn't long before you feel a lurch. Your journey has begun.

As you blast out of the *Victoria* you think about swimming in a large ocean on a new world. You drift and imagine – dolphins can't dream, but they can imagine. Strong images of the sea run through your head, you can almost taste salt water and the silver fish that school within it. These must be memories from your dolphin self. They are soothing things to think about as you hurtle through space toward the water planet.

Abruptly, there is a change in the way the flight feels. The explorer vessel shudders and you can hear a rushing, drumming sound. You've entered the atmosphere of the planet. The hull of the explorer is heating up outside and the metallic feathers that line it will be repelling the heat and keeping you safe inside. There will only be seconds for the robotic control to sense deep water and point the probe towards it.

Insulated in your pod, you don't hear the splash as the explorer drops into the ocean, but you are aware of a change in pressure as you hit the water. The pressure increases as the explorer is propelled into deep water. Then, the little space probe begins to rise again.

"Landing achieved," a robotic voice chirps. Your dolphin sonar tells you it's one of those little bird robots with a long narrow beak. It is taking off the straps that have held it safe on the journey. In the corner a spider-bot detaches itself from the wall too.

"We are scanning the water," a spider-bot tells you. "Please wait for the hatch to release. A location beacon will start shortly. You can follow the sound to come back to make your reports."

The spider-bot turns a valve, opens the hatch and moves upward to avoid the water.

There is a hissing noise as sea water flows into your section of the space ship. A mechanism unzips a hole in the outer casing of the jelly and you swim outside to explore the new world.

The cool water is deliciously full of life. You send out your sonar and it bounces off the sea bottom. You can tell when the water is incredibly deep and where it rises up to form a land mass above the sea. All through the water you feel the creatures of this ocean thriving and swimming about.

You flick your tail and head to the surface, expelling the last of the sleep jelly, ready to take your first breath. As you burst out of the water you inhale the sweet air, flip and dive sideways to circle the explorer. Longtail circles the explorer too. She looks as frisky as you feel. Your instincts are strongly urging you to take off and explore.

The robots have launched a floatation device. It bobs up to the surface. From there they will erect the transmitter. One of the bird-like robots flies into the air and shoots off in the direction of land to get information you won't be able to discover.

It is time to make a decision: Do you:

Want to go and find out what is happening back on the *Victoria*? **P129**

Or

Go with your dolphin friend to explore this world? **P143**

Meanwhile back on the *Victoria*

Nobody tells you to go to sleep again after the dolphins leave the *Victoria*. You are left to yourself and you have fun exploring the ship. You jump on transporters and whizz around the different floors. Little robot birds – hummingbots – follow you around.

The hummingbots show you things by flying ahead after you've asked them a question. That was how you found a galley kitchen and some regular sleep quarters.

It was strange, and even a bit uncomfortable, sleeping in a normal bunk rather than a sleep tank filled with jelly. When you did get to sleep you dreamed you were swimming in a vast ocean. There were strange creatures in the depths and fearsome birds in the air above.

The spaceship is even bigger than you imagined. You haven't even explored half of it when you find a large room filled with sleep tanks like the one you slept in all those years. You expected to find it full of passengers but all the tanks are empty.

"Where are all the people?" you ask a passing service robot.

"One hundred went to a new planet twenty-seven years ago," it says.

That just raises more questions.

"Why didn't everyone get off at the same place?"

"The planet wasn't optimal. It needed help developing the

ecology for human life. A decision was made to send some, not all."

You have one more question. "But why wouldn't everyone wait for a perfect planet to live on?"

"The *Victoria* will not last forever," the service bot answers matter-of-factly. "If some leave for a less suitable planet there are more resources aboard for the rest. It is possible the *Victoria* won't find a suitable planet before the ship is unable to sustain life on-board."

This is a sobering thought. What if you never find a home?

You decide to take more of an interest in the watery planet and stop larking about. You head off to find Dr Alan to get an update.

First you try the dolphin tanks but they are empty and nobody is around. As you are about to leave, a curly-haired kid scoots up and waves cheerily to you.

"Any news about how the dolphins are doing?" she asks.

"I'm looking for Dr Alan to find that out," you say. "Any idea where he is?"

The kid shakes her head. "No, sorry. I'm Grace by the way."

You tell her what you've just found out. "Did you know there have already been settlers sent off the ship?"

"Why would I know anything?" replies your new friend. "Wait, I do know a few things. I seem to know about geology and also the rudiments of thermal energy. Oh, and I know about radio too. I found myself down in an engineering store room the past few days constructing a transmitter just for fun. I suppose I learned all this when I was sleeping. Jolly useful those dreaming caps don't you think? And I can still remember the things I used to know too."

"Like what?" you say. You're not sure you learned anything from the dreaming caps.

"I managed to grow a crop of spuds up on a roof top once. Great things spuds – we're growing them here too you know."

"We are? Where are we doing that?"

"In the hydroponic gardens – haven't you found them? Well, I suppose it's a big place. I asked the hummingbirds to take me to where they grow the food. I've been interested in gardens all my life."

When you tell her that you've even been dreaming about the ocean on the planet below, she looks interested.

"Really? That's a bit of a coincidence then, I've been dreaming about the world down there too. It's like I'm swimming around in the sea. Last time I slept I dreamed about some rough looking fish with sharp teeth and arms. Pretty scary actually."

"That's more than odd then," you say. "I dreamed about the same things. What else did you dream about?"

When Grace talks about using sonar to map the new world you both agree the two of you must be connected to the dolphins in some way when you sleep.

You look at the nearest hummingbot. "Take me to Dr Alan or The Inventor," you say.

The hummingbot flits off down the corridor. You jump on your transporter and get ready to follow. "Oh there's another thing," you say. "The Inventor's mind is in a criminal named Moriarty's body."

She pulls her transporter alongside yours: "Really? That's sinister. Thanks for telling me."

As the two of you zip along after the hummingbot, the corridor changes. Gold ornamentation and fancy scrolling starts to appear around the doorways. The walls are hung with beautiful paintings and there are dazzling lights set into the ceiling.

You pass an alcove with soft padded chairs and a chess board. The alcove looks out to space through a porthole with a large brass frame around it. The doors also have brass labels on them. You pull up outside a door with carvings of different trees and leaves on it. In the middle is the word 'BRIDGE'.

"What would we need a bridge for?" you ask Grace.

She knocks on the door. "It's the word they use for the control room on a spaceship."

This kid has learned everything there is to learn in the sleep jelly by the sound of it. What did you learn you wonder? You don't seem to have any special skills. Your thoughts are interrupted as the door swings open.

The bridge is a large room. Monitors, keyboards, dials and switches are everywhere. Various instruments beep, and lights flicker across screens tracking space outside and things inside the ship.

The far wall is taken up by a window that looks out into space. Through it you see the blue planet.

You never saw Earth from space, when you blasted off, but from the maps you've seen you are fairly sure that the large continents like Europa, Australia and the Americas are much bigger than the islands you can see dotted about on this planet's surface.

"Beautiful isn't it?" says Dr Alan, coming over to greet you. "I'm calling it Atlantica. Unfortunately there isn't much land. The Inventor thinks it's promising though and who knows, perhaps he can devise a way to drain some of it."

"How are the dolphins?" Grace asks.

Dr Alan's eyes move to a receiving station built into one of the consoles. "We know they landed safely and we've had one transmission from the radio station. I'm monitoring them constantly."

He gestures for you to join him at a table in the corner of the room. It is set up with delicate tea cups and a plate of sandwiches. You and Grace fall on the food at once – it's been a while since you ate. Dr Alan eats at a more refined pace. He's probably never eaten with a horde of orphans you think.

"Mmmm, is this fish?" asks Grace.

"Yes," replies the Doctor. "The ship has several tanks, they provide excellent protein and also help with the filtration system by eating little scraps."

"I love fish," you say without thinking. Then you try to remember when you last ate fish. You can't. You've got a memory of chasing after a silver school quite recently but that can't be *your* memory.

You are about to say something when you feel a kick from Grace who must have thought something similar and is telling you to shut up about it.

"Where's the Inventor?" you ask Dr Alan, changing the subject "I expected to find you two working together."

"He's readying supplies and a landing crew should we need it. I've just woken up from a nap. Funny thing, I slept really solidly, you'd think I wouldn't sleep much after all those years in the sleep tank."

That's quite different to you and Grace, you'd had a lot of trouble sleeping. Grace takes a sip of the tea Dr Alan has poured and makes a face as if it tasted awful. When the doctor isn't looking, she spits the tea back into the cup. You decide not to try any.

"If we don't settle on this planet, are there any more nearby?" Grace asks innocently. You watch the Doctor carefully as he answers. He seems fairly relaxed.

"There's another star system about 300 light years away. We want to be sure about this one before we push on."

A buzzing noise and a faint voice distracts Dr Alan from

your conversation. He leaps up and starts tweaking dials. "Hmmm," he says, "Transmission has cut out completely. It could be a problem at either end. The Inventor has the main radio receiver set up in his private rooms. Let's go take a look. Perhaps he got a message from our scouts. There's nothing coming through here."

The three of you head off to find the Inventor. Dr Alan sits on the back of your transporter.

"Jolly useful things these aren't they?" he says. "I say you two, I'm awfully tired. Must be the effects of space travel and waking up. Would you mind dropping me off for a sleep? I'll join you youngsters a bit later."

You find a bunk room and leave Dr Alan to rest. When you get back on your transports Grace directs you to a pump station room. Inside there's the steady noise of water being flushed through pipes.

Grace whispers in your ear through cupped hands. "I don't like this. I think Dr Alan might have been drugged. He didn't seem to know what's going on."

"Yes, very odd." Then you have an idea. "Didn't you say you'd built a radio? Maybe we should check it out."

Grace nods, "It's not far away."

You stop the next service robot that glides into view. Something has been worrying you. "Can you tell me who has the most authority on the ship?"

"The Inventor," the robot states.

"Is there any sort of safety override? What if the Inventor

gave you a command that put people in danger?"

"The Inventor is the final authority," the robot says with simple logic.

After a few turns and a trip down a service lift, you find yourself in a maintenance room full of tools, wires, spare parts and pieces of robotics.

Grace bounds into the room, "Isn't this great?" she enthuses. "When I found all this I spent two days here. Until I got hungry. I'll just flip this switch."

A speaker in the far corner of the room starts making a noise, Grace walks to her radio and starts moving a dial. With less static you figure out you are hearing water – the transmission is coming from under the ocean. Then you hear a few squeals. Oddly you think they mean "Watch out! Crabs."

"Hmm," says Grace, "did you hear that? I mean, did it make sense to you?"

"Crabs," you say, marveling that you understand the language of the dolphins, "Have you heard anything else like that?"

"No, this is the first thing I've heard from the radio, but I've dreamed these voices and I listened for ... oh!"

Another burst of static heralds a change of voice, this time it is a robot voice.

"This is the explorer. The dolphins have detected hostile creatures both on land and sea. The land masses are inhabited by large aggressive carnivorous birds. These birds would pose an ongoing threat to human habitation. Ocean life is very diverse. Some titanium deposits detected. Volcanic activity has potential for geothermal power. The dolphins are hooking the explorer up to a thermal power source now. Current conclusion: Planet not well suited to human habitation due to aggressive native species and limited land for settlement."

You turn to Grace, "Well that's not promising."

A dolphin interrupts the report, their broadcasts must have priority: You get a feeling something is wrong.

The message is faint but you hear the dolphin's words clearly "Do not trust the Inventor."

Your feeling of unease is confirmed. Grace picks up a microphone ready to answer the dolphins but you put a finger to your lips.

Grace hands you a piece of paper and a pencil.

You write: *Careful, The Inventor could be listening.*

Grace writes: *Need to confirm if the Inventor is a danger to ship.*

You write: *Let's investigate.*

Grace picks up the paper and stuffs it in her pocket. The two of you jump on to your 'sporters. Half way down the corridor you come across a hummingbot.

Grace hails the little robot, "Can you tell us where the Inventor is?"

The little machine spends a few seconds communicating with all the other robots. "Sleep Room 4."

"What is he doing?" you ask.

"Imprinting."

"What's that?" Grace asks.

"Transferring the thoughts and memories of one individual to another," the bird reports.

"To make more explorer dolphins?"

"No."

Grace frowns. "What then?"

There is a pause. After half a minute, the little bird says, "Classified," then flies off down the hall.

Grace gives you a confused look. "What is he up to?"

"I'm not sure. What's he copying?"

You ride slowly down the hallway. As you do, you think about what you'd copy if you were Moriarty … then it hits you.

"Himself! He's making copies of himself!"

"Why?"

"Elementary, Grace. He wants to take over. He wants to survive I suppose. He knows what the Inventor knows."

"If only we knew that too."

"Wait," you say, a brainwave hitting you, "maybe we can."

You explain your plan to Grace. As she catches on, her grin grows wider and wider and her head starts nodding.

"Yes, I can get the equipment together," she says. "And I can make the transfer – there's just one problem."

"Leave that to me," you say.

The two of you split up. Grace heads back to her radio room and you go looking for another robot to question.

It isn't long before you find another robot going about its business.

"Where is the Inventor?" you ask.

"In sleep room 4," it answers.

"Not that Inventor, the original, the original record of the Inventor."

"In the library," the robot intones.

"Great!" you say. "Can you show me the way?"

It turns out the library isn't far from the bridge. The room is lined with book-filled shelves from the floor up to the ceiling. There are shelves in the middle of the room too. You haven't seen so many books before, but surely the Inventor's record isn't contained in a book? It must be something else you are looking for.

On one wall you find racks of learning disks, like the ones you've seen attached to sleeping caps. These disks contain lessons on robotics, engineering, agriculture, and all the other skills people need to learn to establish themselves on a new planet. There are languages too, what use will that be you wonder? Then you come to a shelf inscribed with people's names. There are hundreds. Out of curiosity you look for your name and find it in a group labeled 'indentured personnel'. Then another section catches your attention-'criminal minds'. There are only a few files here and a gap exists where Moriarty's file should be. You shudder at the idea of hundreds of Moriarty's.

You quickly scan and find the Inventor's file. You scoop

it up and walk as normally as you can to your 'sporter. You can't help feeling a bit guilty even though you're really sure you are doing the right thing.

Grace has totally reorganized her collection of wires, capacitors, transistors and other electrical components. A bath with a sleeping cap dangling into it, sits in the middle of the room . Grace is pouring sleeping fluid into the bath.

She looks up as you enter. "Good timing! Are you ready for your bath?"

"Do I need one?"

"You need to sleep. That's the only way to overwrite your consciousness."

"I'd better get ready then."

"Are you sure about this?" Grace asks. "There are dangers you know."

"The game's afoot! Besides, what other choice do we have?" you say as you strip down to your underwear and lower yourself into cold sleep jelly. Cold jelly is not as pleasant as warm jelly. You feel a little chill run through you as you go under but when you suck on the breathing apparatus the chill goes and, you are feeling sleepy….

…and then you are coming out of the bath and Grace is there waiting for you with a big grin on her face.

But something is wrong, it's just you. Why can't you feel The Inventor's thoughts? "I don't think it worked Grace, we'll have to try again."

To your surprise Grace laughs and waves a few people

over. There's Dr Alan and someone dressed in a captain's uniform.

"We did it," Grace explains. After you came out of the sleep jelly your subconscious completely accepted the Inventor's mind. You overrode Moriarty's commands and had him sent, with some supplies, to an island on the watery planet.

"Atlantica," interrupts Dr Alan.

"Yes, Atlantica. Anyway he's down there now. It's not that great a place for humans but he should survive. He was going to send a lot of us down there. We've moved on – we're traveling further afield and about to go back to sleep ourselves. The Inventor wanted to give you back your body. And there's more. We've both been promoted. We're no longer indentured. We're toffs!"

Dr Alan interrupts, "Come on you two, let's have a last look at these stars before we go to sleep between them again. I look forward to working with you again in a few hundred years when we reach our next destination."

You look at Atlantica getting smaller. Dr Alan sees an inhospitable planet where the criminal Moriarty is marooned for the rest of his life. You see a planet where an alternate you, in the body of a dolphin, has found a sort of paradise.

Strangely, you and Grace have achieved the thing Moriarty was trying to do. You are both living more than one life. With a part of you swimming below, you wonder if you'll dream of swimming again. You're pretty sure you will.

This part of the story is over. But there are many paths to take. Have you tried them all?

It is time to make another decision. Would you like to:

Go back to the beginning and try another path? **P1**

Or

Go to the List of Choices and find another place to start reading? **P172**

Exploring Atlantica

You have decided to explore while the robots set up the transmitter. That way you'll have information to communicate back to the spaceship sooner.

"Let's head south for a while," you trill to Longtail. "We won't be long."

Using your sonar, you scan the seabed below the explorer. There's a pointy crag down there with warm vibrations coming from it – that should be easy to find again. You can almost smell the forest of seaweed growing around it. Hundreds of little fish and crabs are sheltering from bigger creatures within the seaweed fronds. You'll be able to make a meal from them if you need to, but first you're bursting to explore.

As you swim off you also feel the steady throb of the beacon through the water. You're pretty confident you won't need it but it's an extra way to find your way back.

You and Longtail skim the surface and bounce along the waves. You swim faster and faster enjoying your sleek speedy body. This is better than running, it is more like flying. The contours of the ocean floor are mapped in your head as your sonar bounces off things close and far away. You detect big and small creatures.

Never did you imagine how far a dolphin can 'see'. In the distance you pick up some creatures of a similar size to you.

There is land to one side. It sends nutrients down the

rivers and into the water. These nutrients feed the sea. You can taste the difference in the water. This sense of taste is a little like your human sense of smell but much more specific.

With a burst of speed you arch your back and explode out of the water. Longtail leaps out of the sea right next to you. You hang in the air for a few seconds and look out on the bright sunny day and see birds in the sky. Huge dark birds with wings like bats and long triangular beaks.

"Did you see those birds?" Longtail clicks.

You take another jump out of the water to see what the birds are doing. They are a lot closer.

"Their beaks have teeth," you whistle and click back to Longtail. "Perhaps we shouldn't have drawn attention to ourselves."

You start to panic. The large birds are coming right towards you. You and Longtail dive deep and change direction. It's clear the birds think the two of you will make a good meal. What should you do?

"That's good," says a voice deep in your mind. "Keep scanning for them. You can't sense through the air as well as water, but you should be able to make out something that large."

You don't have time to think about whose the helpful voice is. You just know you want to get away from those big birds.

"Slow down," the voice says, "You can stay under water longer if you use less energy, just stay deep."

Longtail follows as you do what the voice says. The mammoth birds continue circling above. They know you are around somewhere. Diving deeper you disturb a shoal of small fish. The little fish flit and dart and disturb a school of bigger fish. All the movement makes it impossible to sense where the birds are. You start to panic again.

"You're fine," says a voice. "Swim away from the fish. The air creatures will make a meal from the small ones instead."

The voice is right, you've created a distraction by disturbing the shoal. You head further away from land, into the open sea. Behind you the giant birds dive into the water and feast on the fish.

A small blast of sonar finds Longtail swimming in the same direction directly ahead. You risk a quick trip up from the depths to take in some air, barely breaking the surface with your blowhole before you dive down again. Sending out a blast of sonar, you look to see if you've been detected. You are safe. No birds in the area.

Then you remember your mission, explore the world. With a strong kick of your tail, you swim forward, only pausing to taste some delicious small fish those 'air creatures' sent scurrying in your direction.

"Delicious," Longtail clicks as she circles a small school to keep them from darting off into deeper water.

After lunch the two of you head further away from land. Here you start to detect larger life forms. You also pick up on the creatures you sensed before, the ones that were about your size.

"Be cautious, don't enter their territory," the voice warns.

"Who *are* you," you ask. The voice has been quiet since you escaped from the birds. Now that you are out of danger you want some answers.

"I'm the one who was there before you came."

"What?"

"You joined my mind on the great traveling ship."

Now you understand. You're talking to the dolphin, the original inhabitant of the mind you were copied into. It's a reassuring feeling to have this wise soul with you, though you feel like a bit of a trespasser.

"Sorry for invading your mind."

"Don't worry, little one. Together we are exploring this beautiful clean sea. It's a pleasure to have you along. I've enjoyed learning your thoughts."

"What shall I call you?" you ask.

"My pod called me Seeker, because I always sought to find new waters."

"You're living up to your name then," you say.

You and Seeker journey on for a while taking note of the planet and its different creatures.

"We should turn back," Longtail calls.

You start to circle back while reading the map of the sea floor with your sonar. Every time you send out a sonar signal you collect more details, it is like painting a picture in your mind of the undersea landscape. You can sense some of what must be on the land by the taste of the water and by which plant life grows near river mouths. In an area rich with kelp you recognize the last tugs of a strong river, as cool fresh water pours off the land.

"You'll be able to tell them there is fresh water for their steam engines," says Seeker.

Seeker has read your thoughts.

His tone is one of disappointment. "Coal mining makes the sea taste horrible," Seeker says. "Your machines belch smoke and bleed oil and tar. They choke the fish and the creatures of the air."

You suddenly feel sad. This place is so clean, so untouched.

Sensing your distress at the idea of hurting this world, Seeker changes the subject and talks of the long distances he travelled on Earth. Of the many places he visited.

As you swim on, making maps of the ocean, you listen to tales of the southern ocean where men paddling large canoes had driven out the Europeans.

"I know about the Maori savages," you say. "They caused an uprising in the new lands. Britannia used to send prisoners to Australia but the Maori came over and told the Aborigines not to accept any more. After they kicked us out, Maori went on and found coal and gold and other minerals. They became rich. That's why we've had to go out into space."

"The Maori did not seem savage to me," Seeker says. "They kept the sea around them very clean. Britannia fouled the water with all manner of things."

With the giant birds no longer a threat, you think about what Seeker has said. As you do so you drift into a sleepy state. Beside you Longtail does the same. It's a different experience to human sleep. You're semi-conscious and feel part of your brain drift, yet you're never unaware of what is going on around you. Dolphins, you discover, don't really dream but do replay memories. Some of the memories are your own and some belong to Seeker. The memories aren't just sonar pictures but sound and taste too. You find yourself learning about Earth's ocean and how different it is from the sea you are in now. For one thing, this place is cleaner.

You become alert when your sonar picks up two creatures about your size. They are far off but they have abruptly changed course and are coming closer.

You take a breath, remembering how you escaped the big birds by diving, and begin to move away, not too fast to look like you are retreating, just steadily. Mentally you whistle a little tune, like you did back in Londinium when there were street thugs about. An image of walking down cobbled streets flashes into your mind.

"Much as I like to look at your memories, now is not the time to daydream," says Seeker, distracted by your attempt to keep calm.

You feel him checking the creatures with your shared sonar. There is no question now that they are swimming toward you. And they are swimming fast!

It is time to make a decision. Do you:

Swim back to the explorer for shelter? **P156**

Or

Swim further out to sea to seek cover? **P150**

Swim further out to sea to seek cover

You have decided to swim further out to sea. If the creatures mean you harm it would be better to go out to open water rather than risk damaging the space probe.

"I'm heading out into open water," you click to Longtail. "Keep tracking those two large creatures."

"They're following," Longtail clicks in reply.

You send out a burst of sonar to track where you are going. You don't want to lose the location of the space probe. "Just keep moving Longtail."

The ocean beneath you gets deeper and deeper but there are mountains and distinctive currents that make understanding this area in your dolphin mind as easy as if you were gazing at city streets from a high tower. Far below you sense a huge life form moving along with a steady pumping and spurting motion.

"Squid," says Seeker. "It won't bother us. They don't usually come to the surface. Just don't dive too deep for a while."

You come to a large reef and sense another land mass further behind it, perhaps an island. Seeker suggests the reef as a place to hide if needed and suggests you map out some routes through the coral.

You and Longtail take particular note of tunnels through the sharp coral. Toward the centre of the reef your sonar picks up a confusing mass of life forms.

Your followers are close. They may not know there are two of you. You might be able to use that to confuse them. You signal to Longtail to hide in a nearby tunnel. It has a break to the surface where she can breathe.

You swim out of the reef and take another big breath as the creatures come into view.

Their bodies are long and sleek apart from an appendage hanging from each side. The front third of the creature is all mouth and teeth. They look like sharks with arms, and they don't look friendly.

The two creatures split up. For a second you think they are leaving but then you realize it's the way they hunt. They are closing in from two sides like a crab's pincer. When the hunters start moving, you feel your own mind being pushed back and Seeker's taking over.

Seeker speeds toward one of the creatures who opens its toothy mouth ready to take an easy bite. But Seeker deftly swerves, pounds the attacker in the gills with the side of your body and keeps moving towards the reef where he dives into one of the natural tunnels - narrowly avoiding the sharp coral.

Hopefully your pursuer isn't so lucky.

Seeker takes a sharp turn at a fork in the tunnel, blasts a whistle to Longtail and comes back out again. With Seeker's mind in control, you feel like a passenger in a speeding submarine.

Longtail and Seeker surprise the creature you pounded

earlier with another blow to the gills. It's clear this creature is out of the fight. Now it's just you and the other one, but you need air.

Seeker shoots to the surface spreading sonar widely to detect the other creature's location. It isn't far behind but breathing is the most important thing. Seeker propels you out of the water. Your body twists as you change direction and then dives once more. You're clear of the cover of the reef now. Will you be able to outrun the second shark-like creature?

"It's still following you!" Longtail clicks as she streaks up beside you.

Without warning Seeker slows down. You fight your way into his mind in an effort to speed up again.

"More creatures are arriving!" Longtail says.

Oh no - this is it, the hunters are closing in. Why don't they come in for the kill? Perhaps Longtail will still be able to get back to the ship if they attack you.

"Save yourself Longtail!" you whistle. "I'll try to hold them back. Swim for it!"

"You're brave but a bit stupid," says Longtail. "Pay attention."

"Slow down," Seeker says, "Friends have come."

And it's true. Newcomers are swimming with you. Your pursuer flees, chased away by some of these new dolphins. You slow, take a fresh breath, and try to get your heart to stop pounding.

The newcomers take turns to swim close. You study them too. They are very much like your dolphin-self, air breathing mammals that use sonar and are able to sing the high pitched noises that form a basic language.

They are singing you a welcoming song. You listen and join in when you recognize a part that repeats. Pretty soon you and Longtail are singing in unison with the other dolphins. The song has connected you and you start to understand each other.

"Where did you come from?" you ask one of the pod.

"Inside the reef," she says.

You remember that mass of life you detected. The pod must have been clustered inside a cavern in the reef. When they heard you call to Longtail they came to your rescue.

You travel with the others for many days. You map and explore great tracts of the ocean. You find that the huge birds that you met on your first day nest along every rocky outcrop and feed upon sea creatures. They do not fly far out to sea and they can't fly in bad weather. You doubt they'd get on well with humans.

Your new pod have a very wide territory. Whenever it is your turn to guide the pod you lead them back towards the explorer. Before long the others realize there is somewhere you want to go and are content to go along.

Eventually you return to the explorer with its robot escort.

As you approach the floating vessel, Seeker speaks to you

directly. For the last few days the two of you have acted as one and you had almost forgotten you were two separate minds.

"Are you going to tell the humans that this is a good place to come to, or say it is a bad place for them?"

You hadn't really thought about it like that. You just know that you need to make a report so they can decide. You remember the time you passed the river mouth and Seeker noted how clean and fresh the water was. You think back to the river Thames in Londinium – its waters would be fouled and polluted when they reached the ocean. If the *Victoria* lands here there will be changes everywhere. The sea will be a major source of food for the new settlers and they will want to get rid of anything that threatens them. You don't like those big birds on the cliff but now you know not to make yourself a target, they can't harm you. You aren't fond of the shark creatures but you are safe from them in your pod. You know they have a role to play in the ocean.

Seeker has been following your thoughts. "You must tell the humans what you think is best for them to know."

It is night. The big birds don't fly at night so the pod comes close to shore to sing. Phosphorescence covers their bodies and they shine in the water along with hundreds of other creatures. Out of the water comes a mammoth animal. The dolphins have sung it up from the depths as the moon hangs low over the planet and the tide pulls toward it. On the cliffs the birds raise their heads and sing too. By day they are fierce, but now, on this moonlit night, their humming choir makes an operatic contribution as it echoes off the cliffs.

You swim inside the space ship where two robots sit waiting to help you with the transmitter. You nudge the 'transmit' button with your nose and send your report.

Planet not suitable for human habitation.

Outside the explorer, you hear your friends and the great ocean singing. Beyond the moon twinkle millions of stars. One of those will surely make a suitable home for those on the *Victoria*.

Moments later, the *Victoria* fires its engines and, like a comet, streak off across the sky returning to its quest of finding a home.

You, on the other hand, are home. You exit the explorer, swim at top speed, then leap from the water, twirling in the air before you splash down. Then you raise your voice and sing.

You have come to the end of this part of the story. Do you:

Go back to the beginning and try another path? **P1**

Or

Go to the list of choices and pick another place to begin reading? **P172**

Swim back to the space probe for shelter

You don't know what those creatures were, so it seems safest to get back to the explorer and check on the transmitter. You have things to report now. You know a little about the waters, you've discovered giant birds, but most importantly, you need to warn the crew on the *Victoria* that the Inventor might not be safe from the criminal whose mind he took over.

"My mind was dormant, until a moment of great stress," says Seeker, reading your thoughts. "If this bad person is the same, he may return to consciousness too and not want to share his body."

Seeker has a good point, but as you swim back you notice that the creatures are still coming your way. You don't have time to worry about the Inventor right now.

If these creatures mean you harm, you can swim inside the explorer and close the hatch. Longtail chirps in agreement about the direction you've taken. She's picked up the creatures with her sonar too and you know she'd prefer not to take a risk.

Soon you sense the warm mountain on the sea floor, and not long after that, you hear the *ping* of the beacon. Are the creatures attracted to the beacon too?

The top half of the explorer is bobbing above the surface, but the tunnel you exited from is submerged and ready for you to enter. You both speed inside. Longtail activates the door closer with her nose just as you catch a glimpse of two long shapes speeding toward the opening. You hit the LOCK button and then relax when you hear a satisfying *clunk*.

You swim up a level and look out through a porthole. Two black fish are now circling the pod. They have the huge eyes of creatures that spend a lot of time in deep water. They also have arms.

One of them takes a run at the porthole and attempts to smash it open. When it fails the second one tries biting at the window and ripping at the outer coverings with webbed fingers. You stare into a large open mouth spread over the porthole. Several sets of jagged teeth, one behind the next, glisten in the light emitted from the explorer.

You and Longtail watch in horror as webbed hands scrape and grasp at the porthole.

Longtail sends frightened clicks and whistles.

You reply with strong blasts of reassurance. "If the explorer kept us safe through space it will withstand this."

You're almost positive, but then you don't really know what these creatures are capable of. Around you, the explorer clanks and clangs as the predators try to break into it. Thankfully the feathered hull repels the attack but you can't stay inside forever and for the first time since landing on the water planet you wish you hadn't accepted the crazy adventure you're undertaking.

You swim to another porthole and watch the creatures

outside. They stop bashing at the hull and swim in lazy circles around your vessel. You swim upward to take a breath. Thank goodness the explorer is set up to house the robots above, and there's a pocket of air where you can breathe safely. When you look up, you see a large clear ring set into the top of the small craft. You can see the sky.

A robot opens the roof and sends out a hummingbot. It must be going to scan the creatures swimming around your craft.

You haven't seen the dry area of the explorer before – the robots have been very busy. You knew they were going to erect a radio transceiver but it looks like a lot more is going on. Beyond the wet area where you surfaced, you see sparks from welding and building.

Several flying robots approach when they see you. One carries a radio microphone. It wants you to make a report.

The other makes an announcement to you both: "You left the explorer without armor and tracking equipment. You must put on your armor in case of hostile native activity. You must wear your tracking device to gather information about the planet."

You wonder if the robots have realized you've brought some hostile natives back to the explorer with you and whether armor will be enough to help you defend yourself against them.

"Please come out of the water and onto the dock," says the bird. You submerge and swim back down the way you came. When you are almost back to the locked sea door you set off with speed so you can propel yourself out of the water and onto the dock mounted just above water level.

The creatures outside pick up your movements and become more alert as they see you swimming about inside the explorer.

With a splash and a flop, you land on the dock. Then you hear banging and tapping on the hull again. The creatures are not giving up.

The nice thing about robots is they aren't emotional. Humans would have given you a lecture about how bad it is to leave without being fully equipped, but the robots are all business. You can't help feeling a little guilty though. If you hadn't made it back here the mission would have failed and you also wouldn't be able to report about the consciousness of your host animal.

The microphone is slung over a rafter and hangs in front of you.

"Please report. We know the explorer has landed safely. What can you tell us about the planet? Over."

Longtail begins to make a report – she squeaks and trills into the microphone. Her human counterpart should be able to interpret what she says. She explains about the large birds. She talks about the warm water and something under the ground. You didn't really put it together but Longtail understands there's some kind of underwater volcano — there might be earthquakes she tells them. She's noticed all sorts of things.

"This is Seeker," you say, and pause in case anyone answers you. There is no answer though – it must take some time for your transmission to reach the *Victoria*. You describe everything you have discovered so far.

Every so often there is a clang from the creatures outside. You tell the people on the space ship far above you what the creatures are like. Then you tell them about your experience with your dolphin mind, how it's awake and just as much in control of its body as you are.

"I can speak with the dolphin mind, but sometimes it takes over – for instance when the bird predators attacked us. We may share this body but the host's mind is not dormant like you told me. Repeat. The host is not asleep and it can take control. Did you hear me?"

There is a sudden click and the transmitter is silent. Without the noises of the transmission you hear water lapping on the dock and the occasional clang of the creatures outside.

Three robots set to work trying to re-connect it, but after a while they stop. One of them perches on the microphone looking down on you.

"What is the problem?" Longtail asks.

"The problem is not at this end. We must wait until the *Victoria* is receiving again," one hummingbot chirps.

"What could have caused the disconnection?" you ask.

"Sunspots or solar flares possibly, or mechanical failure."

"Longtail," you say, "is your human brain the only mind operating in there – or is your dolphin mind awake too?"

"We're both here, Seeker."

"Let's leave another message for the *Victoria*. We need to make sure they understand the significance of the host's mind being active Then we need to get rid of the monsters outside."

"I'm frightened," trills Longtail.

"Don't worry. The bots will sort something out," you say.

And perhaps you are right because the robots bring a fine chainmail sheath toward you and slip it over most of your body. You can feel little electrodes activating against your skin. It is surprisingly lightweight, like the fine leather gloves rich ladies had back in Londinium. You once got tipped half a crown when you returned a glove that had been dropped on the street. It felt soft and warm in your hand as you raced after the carriage to return it hoping for a reward.

"Won't I rust in this?" you ask, imagining yourself rusted up at the bottom of the ocean.

"No, your armor is a titanium alloy," the hummer above you reports, "It won't rust."

Woven inside the armor is something not unlike the sleeping cap you wore on the ship.

"Why do I need a sleeping cap?"

"It won't send you to sleep, it will read your brain impulses and help you. You can make broadcasts back to the explorer."

You ease back into the water and swim around, trying out the armor like a new pair of shoes. You feel a little heavier but also stronger. You pause at a porthole looking for the mean toothed fish. All you can see is the light filtering down from above, so you send out a blast of sonar. You get crystal clear images this time – it must be something to do with the armor, a built-in antenna perhaps.

When your sonar bounces back, you see that the predators are swimming away from the explorer at speed. Has something else caught their attention?

You look at Longtail and she gives a nod. The nod strikes you as a very human response but you know she's suggesting you head back outside.

Once in the ocean you make a few quick turns, ready to head back inside if you feel encumbered by the armor. To your surprise it fits very well and doesn't slow you down. With a burst of speed, you venture out further.

Another blast of sonar tells you there's no danger about. The amplifying effect of your suit means you can read things in the air. You pick up a small gull wheeling in the sky above.

This means you'll be able to spot the large birds too! A small fish scoots by and you put on a burst of speed to catch it.

Your suit gives you a boost of power and you shoot past the startled fish. Longtail surges past you too and for a while you're both racing about showing off your new powers. This is great, you'll be able to out run those horrible creatures if, or when, they return. Suddenly you're incredibly hungry and you feast on fish and small squid.

After the meal you try some jumps. You surge out of the water and find Longtail jumping over you. In the distance one of those large birds is cruising in the sky and moves toward you. Now you are so fast you decide you won't run. You jump again teasing it, but it doesn't come much closer and you wonder why.

"They might not want to be too far from the cliffs," speculates Longtail.

She might be right, but before you can experiment with what distance the big birds are willing to go out to sea you get a message from the explorer.

"Please survey the volcanic activity below."

You and Longtail take another huge leap out of the water and make a teasing flip at the faraway birds then dive.

You soon realize the suit lets you to go much deeper than normal. It is protecting you against the water pressure and helping boost your oxygen levels.

"These gadgets are wonderful," says Seeker. "I've never been this deep before."

You're glad Seeker feels that way. He might have felt horribly used, but his adventurous spirit means that he sees the enhancements the robots have given you as a way to do more exploring.

You've learned more about space and other animals on

this journey than you ever expected. Until now, you never realized how intelligent another creature could be.

You dive into deeper and darker shades of blue until the water around you is the color of midnight. Mountainous shapes below glow red and orange, as lava oozes from their vents.

"Please describe what you're seeing," instructs a voice in your cap.

Beside you Longtail makes her report. She tells the robots on the explorer that the water is getting warmer, which it is, and that there is a glow from the lava in the depths. She says there are 'multiple fissures' and you wonder what those might be, probably the little volcanoes. It seems the human part of Longtail has knowledge of geology that you don't have.

You circle the volcanic area. There are craggy looking fish everywhere and the bottom is alive with crabs and the long tendrils of swaying seaweed. You see a crab nimbly step away from some hot lava but unfortunately it moves into the path of a creature with tentacles the same color as the seabed.

The crab is gobbled up in seconds.

"Return to the explorer. Your next task is to hook a cable to the steam vents. We can generate some power for the explorer."

Longtail swishes upward to go get the cable. You turn and follow her, passing by a tall lava formation that towers up higher than the rest.

Just as you pass the lava tower there's a sharp jolt and you feel yourself held back. Something has hold of your tail.

You twist around and see that the tower wasn't a rock at all. It's actually a rock creature. You beat your tail, but can't break free.

Are you going to be its next meal?

You beat your tail once more and stare toward the surface. Longtail is a disappearing shadow in the glimmer of the world far above. The grip on your tail grows tighter as you thrash about in panic. You'll need more air very soon. If you don't do something to get free you'll die.

Then you hear the spider-bot. "Use the laser."

Laser? What laser?

Seeker's voice comes through, as it always does in moments of stress, "Let's try out some human gadgets!"

There is a sudden hum and a beam of white light comes out of your helmet. Wherever you look, the beam follows. You direct the laser toward the rock creature. It cuts through the tentacle holding you and the creature lets go.

You shoot upward with your lungs pounding for fresh air.

Longtail meets you on the surface and brushes her body up against yours. She feels smooth and warm and reassuring.

"Your tail!" she exclaims.

Glancing back you see ragged cuts along its length. You shudder as you think about what might have happened if you'd been permanently injured. Any more damage to your tail would mean you couldn't swim.

You explain about the rock creatures to Longtail and how you used the laser to free yourself.

"It will be a great deterrent against those big fish," you say. "They won't want to mess with us."

Longtail agrees but says we also need to learn to get along. "I love it here and I've been worried about the big fish, but we need to find a way to live alongside them. If we only use strength and power we won't ever be friends. Perhaps they are intelligent too and we need to find a way to speak with them."

The robots insist you return to the explorer to get your tail looked at.

Longtail will make another report to the *Victoria*. You re-enter the explorer and go up to the deck. The spider-bots gently take off your armor. You feel a little lighter with it off and are surprised to find yourself looking forward to wearing it again – its proved itself very useful. Soon you're getting a full medical from the spider-bots who treat your wounds and check for infection.

They say you won't have any natural immunity to any microbes the rock creature might have passed on through your cuts. Despite the bots patching you up, you have mixed feelings about them.

Robots displaced a lot of workers on Earth and led to hunger and crime. They could have led to a better life for everyone, but they were taken over by the rich. Perhaps in a new world people will use robots to make things better for everyone.

The robots finish checking you over and say you should both rest before taking the cable down to hook up to the volcano.

"I can do it on my own," Longtail says.

"Don't you dare!" you say. "There are too many dangers out there. Even with our new armor I think we need to stick together."

"That's right," says Seeker. "Always act as a pod."

The next day a hummingbot flies through the port in the top of the explorer. The spider-bots check the bird over for damage. They apply oil to its joints so it can keep working in the harsh sea air. Once its maintenance is taken care of it reports that it has found several islands but they are all quite small.

"There might be a way to build bridges between some of the islands over time. Settlers will have a tough time here though," Longtail muses.

It's a pity everyone can't become a dolphin you think, this place is pretty good if you are a swimmer.

The next day you and Longtail take the power cable down to the underwater volcano. You take care not to swim close to the rock crabs now you know what they are. Just as the pair of you have finished connecting the cable you notice shadows above you. It's the vicious fish who chased you … and there are lots of them!

Longtail blasts some sonar to check where they are. They are close but they don't seem to be coming any nearer. Something else has their attention. You pick up a faint sonic cry. It sounds like a distress call from a youngster.

Dozens of sharky voices answer. One croons softly and sounds just as distressed. Something tells you that it is the mother whose baby is in trouble.

The shark fish don't seem to be able to help the baby – they are circling above but unwilling to dive down.

"The baby must be caught by one of the rock crabs," says Longtail.

You were thinking the same thing.

"Let's help," Longtail says.

With your new armor you might be able to help, but you can't help thinking these creatures wanted to kill you not long ago.

The baby gives another cry, fainter this time.

Longtail doesn't wait, she takes off toward the noise.

"Let's help," says Seeker.

So you follow. At least you can look out for Longtail. You come to a shelf in the ocean where it suddenly gets very deep. A forest of crab spires pokes out of the deep. Near the top of one of these you can see a small shark fish weakly pulling to try to free itself. You know just what that feels like.

The shark people swim above the crabs. Occasionally one of them swims overhead with a rock in its hands and tries to aim at the crab arms. It is trying to hit them. Other crab limbs have formed a sort of net above the baby though and the rocks aren't getting through.

The shark people have noticed you now. You don't know what they are thinking. There are perhaps twenty of them. If you don't rescue their baby you don't like to think what they'll do.

Longtail gets as close as she can to the baby and carefully activates her laser. You circle around above her, vulnerable now to an attack by the shark folk. You hope they realize you are there to help. You activate your own laser and one by one the smaller crabs over the top of the baby pull away. Now Longtail goes closer and works on the arm holding the baby.

The baby is barely moving now. It is almost out of air.

A rock crab claw moves toward Longtail and you give it a blast. It recoils back into the crevice. With a *crack!* the arm holding the baby breaks and the little one drifts upward then stops, too weak to swim.

Longtail dives underneath braving the rock crabs and nudges the baby up toward the surface. You give short laser blasts to the area beneath her and then, as she comes level with you, you join her in nursing the baby upwards. As you clear the danger area, all the shark people race toward you and you brace yourself for a fight.

The mother of the baby gets there first. She is crooning and joins you to bring her baby to the surface. The others swim nearby, focused on the little one. When the baby takes a breath it starts to wriggle and then swim. It comes back to Longtail and nudges at her, making little chirruping noises and then swims to its mother who repeats the noises. Silently, the rest of the shark people swim past and then move off. The mother and baby are the last to go.

"I don't think we'll have any more problems from them," you say to Longtail.

"I hope they'll be kind to our children," she says.

"What?" you say. It's true that Longtail has been getting pudgier by the day but you just thought it was all that fish she was eating.

You haven't felt lonely for a second on this adventure but the thought of having a new member of your pod makes you launch yourself out of the water and twirl in the air. How lucky you are to be a dolphin.

"What should we call the baby, do you think?" asks Longtail.

"How about Victoria if it's a girl?" you say. "Victoria Oceanborn."

"Perhaps," says Longtail. "In that case perhaps Victor for a boy?"

You swim back to the explorer and get the bots to turn on the radio.

"Come in *Victoria*. I have exciting news."

You have reached the end of this section of the story. Do you:

Find out what happened back on The Victoria? **P129**

Or

Find out what would have happened if you had not swum back to the explorer? **P150**

Or

Go to the List of Choices and pick another place to start reading? **P172**

Or

Go back to the very beginning and start over? **P1**

List of Choices

More You Say Which Way Adventures

Pirate Island

Volcano of Fire

Lost In Lion Country

Once Upon an Island

In the Magician's House

Secrets of Glass Mountain

Danger on Dolphin Island

The Sorcerer's Maze - Jungle Trek

The Sorcerer's Maze - Adventure Quiz

YouSayWhichWay.com

Made in the USA
Coppell, TX
29 January 2020